KATIE DEE & KATIE HAW

To Ms Russel's
CLASS —
Hope you enjoy
the stories!
Jes Roe

KATIE DEE

AND

KATIE HAW

Letters From A Texas Farm Girl

A Novel by

JOE REESE

Illustrations by
Melissa Britton James

COTTEN PUBLISHING CO.

For Pam

Published by
Cotten Publishing Co.
P. O. Box 1338
Lubbock, Texas 79408

ISBN: 0-925854-29-8

Printed and bound in the United States of America

First Printing: February 1995

Second Printing: October 2003

Third Printing: June 2007

Katie Dee & Katie Haw

Possum

Possum

Dear Katie Dee,

Our year didn't begin so great. I left the door open out into the yard and—well, I better begin farther back.

My job when we get home from school is, I have to feed the beagles. Mama and I always stop at the grocery store in Midlothian after school. Mr. Smith is the butcher. He puts leavings of meat and bones in a big pasteboard box and we carry the box home in the back of the truck. The beagles go just about nuts when we roll up in the driveway. Anyway, this day I took the meat scraps to the mud room door, and Mama went in the front door to put her school papers away. Spud and Annie were jumping all over me, so I kind of tipped the box over getting the scraps out and blood ran all over my shoes, which the dogs sniffed like I thought they were going to eat them.

Finally I got about half of the meat put out but it was so cold I left the door kind of open.

That caused the problem.

Outside it had begun to rain. It was gray and cold, a typical crummy January day. I mean, like, January has New Year's Day and all, and the bowl games, which the Aggies still aren't in one of them, but it still isn't much of a month.

"Somebody ought to close the front porch door," Mama said.

I just stood there. Then I got a paring knife out of the drawer and started peeling potatoes with her.

1

I don't know why I didn't do like she said.

"You get the dogs fed?"

"Uh huh."

"Then you fry the potatoes and make us a little salad. I'll go down and feed the sheep."

"All right."

I cooked like she asked me to. Then we ate and washed dishes. Then we went in the living room and she graded papers and I wrote my report on the indians of Tierra del Fuego which was harder than I thought it was going to be. I mean, last week it was easy to write about the principal products of Ecuador because Ecuador is so big. Soybeans and hemp and shellfish and phosphate and teak—lots of stuff—so you can easy get three pages, or even more. But Tierra del Fuego's principal product is just seals.

I don't think I would like to live there.

It took me an hour and a half to finish it. Then I said goodnight to Mama and walked down the hall to my room. Then I opened the door and saw a possum on my desk.

The possum looked up at me. He bared back his cheeks so that you could see his gums and teeth; then he flattened out and hunched back against the window and went:

Hissssssssss.

I closed the door, walked back through Mama's bedroom, back down the hall, and into the living room. She had changed into her nightgown and was peering down kind of half over her glasses, and had that kind of ferocious look she gets when she grades papers. She was writing with a red pen, bearing down so hard that you could hear the paper almost ripping.

"Mama!"

"Yes, dear?"

"There's a possum in my room!"

She looked up. Then she straightened her glasses and kind of shook her head like a dog shakes all over when it climbs out of a lake you've thrown it into.

She always has to do that when she stops grading.

"What did you say?"

"I said there's a possum in my room!"

She got up then and put her hands on my shoulders and looked down at me, kind of like she was getting ready to grade *me.*

"There's a possum actually *in* your *room?*"

"Yes!"

"How did it get there?"

"I don't know!"

So we walked together down the hall and through her room. I was standing close to her with my arm around her waist.

She opened the door.

The possum was still on the desk.

It kind of bared its gums and teeth again, and flattened out and backed up against the window. Then it went:

Hissssssss.

"See!"

We both knew what the possum was doing on my desk in particular, because, like, I have this problem about leaving food on my desk and—I don't really want to go into that. You know how it is.

"Well," she said, "we just have to get the thing out."

"How? Can we call somebody?"

"Who?"

"I don't know."

"Me neither. Come on."

We went to the pantry and got a broom. Then we went back to my room. The possum hadn't moved.

3

"I'm going to—I don't know—kind of herd the possum off the desk and make it run out onto the porch. Once it's on the porch it'll see the open door and go outside."

"All right."

We opened the door and walked into the room and around my bed. The possum just kind of glared at us. The only light in the room was my reading light and the possum's eyes glowing green. Mama walked fast up by the closet so she could reach my desk with the broom.

She lifted the broom and whacked at it two or three times on the desk.

"Hyaaahhh! Hyaaahhh! Go Possum! Go Possum! Hyaaahhh. Hyaaahhh!"

Whackwhackwhack!

Whackwhackwhack!

"Hyaaahhh! Hyaaah!"

Some of the papers I had been tracing on, as well as the wax paper a cheese sandwich had come in and was still kind of wrapped in—and, I guess, part of the sandwich itself, as well as part of a devil's food Hostess Cup Cake—all flew up into the air and out into the room because the straw fat part of the broom was making a tornado when it went up and came down and went up and came down.

The possum backed up against the window and looked kind of bewildered at the broom, like it was a flying saucer landing again and again and again and for a minute he just was hypnotized.

But he didn't move. Except to kind of shift his weight from one front paw to the other and flatten out a little more so that he looked like those kids' book pictures of Mr. Hedgehog. Not hissing so much this time but just staring at us with a wide open mouth all cottony inside.

"Maybe he's playing possum," I said.

"No, he's not 'playing possum.'"

"What are you going to do?"

"I'm going to get him off of that desk. I want that possum out of this house. Now get back. When he comes off of there I don't want him biting you."

She changed ends of the broom so this time she was holding the fat straw part. Then she stepped out a little farther into the room, so that she could get the broom handle between the possum and the window. Then she—Mama is very strong and you could see the muscles in her arm—just kind of slid the possum over the top of my desk, toward the edge.

"Get off there! Get off there!"

"You're getting him, Mama!"

"You! Get off there, possum. Go! Go!"

Suddenly it dove off the desk and hit the wooden floor with its claws going like, really *fast*, and careened off the side of my dresser and skidded right by the porch door and blammed into the side of my trunk where I keep toys and stuffed animals and then kind of got right again and waddled in a woozy way through into Mama's bedroom.

We got to the door just in time to see its pink tail disappearing under her bed.

"Darn!" said Mama real loud.

Except, that isn't what she really said. But I'm not allowed to write what she really said. And you probably aren't allowed to read it either.

We just stood there.

The possum was under Mama's bed, not moving.

After a while we walked over toward the bed. Both of us bent down and looked. You could see those green eyes glaring back at us. He was all the way under the bed, way back, hunched up against the wall.

"Darn," Mama said again, kind of out of breath (see what I wrote above), just looking at the possum like this had become something very personal between the two of them.

"What do we do now?"

"We get it out of there. Don't ask me how. We'll have to prod it out. Then we'll—I don't know—kind of channel it down the hallway and out of the house."

So we made a plan. While she stayed by the bed, sitting squatted with the broom in her hand, ready if the possum should panic and make a run for it who knows where, I did what I was told, trying to figure out if anything could go wrong. I didn't see a way. The first door down the hall, on the right, was the one to the bathroom. I shut it. I even turned the light out so the possum wouldn't see that it was a bathroom and for some crazy possum reason want to go in. Next I went on down the hall and shut the living room door on the left. Same thing, turned out the lights. Mama had banked the fire, so that a bed of ashes lay over the coals. Other than a few little points of fire, there was no light in the room. Then I opened the door from the kitchen to the porch. Then I opened the door from the porch to the outside, and propped it with a brick. You could hear the wind moaning and whipping through the kitchen. It was really cold now.

When I got back she was ready.

"You got them all closed?"

"Right."

"Are we ready?"

"We're ready."

"All right. Come and stand over here by me."

I did.

She reached as far as she could under the bed. I couldn't see anything, but you could hear scuffling and hissing and grunting and more scuffling and the sound of the broomstick raking against the bedsprings. Then more scuffling and hissing and soft thudding of the stick poking into the possum and then nothing except the possum breathing hard and being slid along the floor and Mama breathing hard and working her way toward the end of the bed.

Finally the possum came out.

He didn't really shoot out like I thought he would. He came out kind of tired, swishing that tightwhiterope tail over the floor, looking up at the ceiling light and then over at the window like he was looking for another possum to check with and see if he was doing the right thing. And then with Mama yelling at him and whackwhackwhacking the broom down on the floor right beside of him, first to the right and then to the left, he waddled on out of the bedroom and into the hall.

Just like we wanted.

On down the hall.

It was working.

As he went on down the hall he picked up speed. By the time he reached the kitchen he was moving pretty fast, which made me feel confident about the situation and how it would come out, until a—I don't know—I guess you'd have to call it a revelation. Something like a revelation hit me, and I realized what I'd done. Because, when I opened the door from the back porch outside, I should have remembered that the meat scraps were still there on the porch, and that Spud and Annie would hear the door opening and smell the scraps and come in and start eating them.

Which is what they had done of course and which is why they were right there, getting all covered with blood and worked into a hound dog feeding frenzy when they saw the possum as it came skidding into the kitchen and banking right to head for the porch.

There are some things, Katie Dee, that are just very hard to describe with only the words that we use in our regular language.

What I can say is this: there was one moment when everyone—Mama, me, the possum, Spud, and Annie—were just *real* still. That was the moment it took for Mama to realize that Spud and Annie were there, and for me to remember that Spud and Annie were there, and for the possum to realize that Spud and Annie were there and were dogs, and for Spud and Annie to see the possum.

That moment probably lasted about a million million millionth of a second.

After that moment was over, things began to happen very very fast, and it would probably take one of those writers who write books for the library to describe it. The best I can do is this: imagine if you had a basketball (because that was about how big the possum was) and you lathered it all over with glue and dumped it again and again into a big barrel filled with chicken feathers, except gray instead of white. Then you made sure the basketball was pumped up so tight it was ready to explode, so it would bounce real high even if you just dropped it by accident on a cement floor. And then you found this huge man and you put him in a concrete room that was maybe four or five feet square. And you told him to take the ball and just *hurl* it and *hurl* it and *hurl* it and see what happens.

I don't know how long all that lasted. Probably not very long. But it seemed like it lasted real long.

There was a point though when I thought, "It can't get much worse than this," and so I was surprised when the possum and the dogs, since they had careened off every other possible place in the room, finally careened over against the swinging door that led into the living room and so that's where the possum found itself—and Spud and Annie too, of course. Looking back on the whole thing, here's the only part I don't understand. I mean, I understand why the possum came into the house and I understand why it went into my room. I understand why it went under the bed and why Spud and Annie were on the back porch and why they chased the possum into the living room.

What I don't understand is why the possum ran into the fireplace.

The only thing I can imagine is that it was so dark and square shaped that to the possum it must have looked like a door leading outside.

Anyway, when the possum rammed into the bed of ashes there was a kind of "whummmmp," as though someone had dropped a hundred pound block of cement down the chimney, and a cloud of ashes and burning coals exploded out into the room, where the coals started making little black smoking holes in the rug, which, after not much time at all, you could smell burning.

As for the possum, Mama and I have different memories of that. Mama says that the possum screamed. I don't think possums know how to scream, and I say she was the one that screamed. She says she's not the kind of person that screams. I don't know. I do know the possum jumped straight up so it looked like it was being sucked up into the chimney by a huge vacuum cleaner. It even disappeared for just a second and when it came back down there was another "whummmp," and more ashes and coals flew out into the room, this time along with the possum, which we kind of forgot about because the rug was on fire.

"Mama! It's burning!"

9

"Get the dogs! Get the dogs!"

"The rug is burning!"

"Get the dogs! Get the dogs!"

Somehow I was able to do that, maybe because they were just running between my legs. It was a miracle—kind of like catching two very fast ground balls at the same time when you aren't wearing a glove. But I got my fingers around both of their collars and heaved and tugged and pulled until I got them out onto the front porch and I could slam the door behind them.

When I got back I saw her stamping out little fires on the rug and the possum waddling out from under the couch and into the hall. She says that a coal had landed over by the couch and was making the couch smoke. I say the smoke was coming from the possum.

Like I said before, there are things we don't remember the same way.

So I helped Mama put out the fires and then we swept what we could of the ashes off the hearth and rug and couch and magazine stand and coffee table and big chair and curtains and corner bookshelves and ivy plant and window sill.

Then we went into her bedroom, and bent down.

The possum had gotten under her bed again. It was back where it had been before, just staring out at us.

She got up and kind of pulled me up and said, "Go to bed."

"Mama," I said, "how are we going to get the possum out?"

"I don't care. I'm tired. It has not been a good day."

"But where are you going to sleep?"

"Here. This is my bed."

"There's a possum under it!"

"I know."

"You can't sleep with a possum."

"I've slept with worse."

And then she kind of dove on the bed, and didn't even move, and it seemed like within a few seconds she was asleep.

So I went into my room and said my prayers and lay down and knew I wasn't going to sleep, but did, so I must have been tired too.

When we woke up the next morning the possum was gone.

I don't know where he went or how he got out of the house.

I also don't know what Mama meant about having slept with worse than a possum.

How could you sleep with anything worse than a possum?

I guess that's one of those things I'll learn when I grow up. I'm not looking forward to it.

Forever yours,

Katie Haw

The Smile of
Melting Snow

The Smile of Melting Snow

February 5, 1967
Midlothian, Texas

Finally we got snow, Katie Dee.

It began in the afternoon about two o'clock. Just a few flakes at first. But it thickened up fast, and Mrs. Bergvall had trouble making people stay in their desks. We all kept looking out of the wall of windows on the north side of the building, wanting to run over and look out into the street to see if the flakes were sticking.

By the time Mama picked me up it was a white world. We could barely see driving home. The windshield wipers made that sound that lulls you into a trance, and it seemed like driving in a cloud.

We got into the house, changed clothes, and went down to the barn to put up the sheep. It was one of those days when you work and don't talk. I put out the oats while she walked down to the creek to get the few sheep still down there.

It took three trips from the bin to get all the troughs full. I had made two of them when she got back from the creek to help me. It was murky dark, snow whirling and the wind starting to howl around the corners of the barn. We filled the lambs' trough last; it's like a jail, except instead of bars there are wooden slats four inches wide, each slat about a foot apart. The ewes can't get through the space, but the lambs can. As they grow we shave the sides of the slats to make the openings bigger, so they can always just barely squeeze through.

When Mama opened the gate leading out to the pasture it was like a buffalosheep stampede, a million waist-high sacks of wet wool thundering across the lot. One of the big lambs that weighed almost a hundred pounds got stuck between two slats. I rammed my shoulder against his tailbone and tried to force him through. I couldn't do it, though. He was really stuck.

"Mama!"

She had started back around the corner of the barn, on her way to close the gate into the pasture.

"Mama!"

"What?"

"Lamb stuck!"

We pushed together hard and finally that old lamb slipped on through with a kind of "ssshuup!" sound, spraying water back on us as though we had been squeezing out a fatlamb sponge.

We sat there for a minute getting our breath. Bob Burton's Angus cows stared at us from his pasture across the road. You could barely see them in the snow. They looked like black inkblobs on white posterboard.

Then we walked back to the house.

Mama took care of dinner while I built the fire. She had the easy job; there had been a roast in the oven all day and the smell of the gravy and onions filled the house. She just had to make a salad. The fire was hard because the kindling had gotten wet. I had to search out the driest twigs I could find from the bottom of the box on the porch. Even then it took some blowing, but finally a flame began to crackle in the stick teepee. Soon smoke was twisting fast up the chimney and I could put in some bigger wood. The water was hissing on the black-wet bark.

Outside it was pitch dark. The Hall's yard light, way over across the creek, glowed — a bluish spot no bigger than a star.

We ate in the living room by the light of the fire. Every now and then you could hear a railroad whistle through the howling of the wind.

I helped with the dishes, and later on worked on my geography and math.

Then I went to bed. The room was cold but I have the best thick blankets in the world, with a space hollowed out for Bunny. I read for a while. Mama had turned the radio on in the kitchen. You could hear a woman singing soft, with a guitar in the background. With that and the sound of the snowstorm and Bunny, it was easy to go to sleep.

I don't know what woke me up. I'm not sure if it was the banging of the rifle against the closet door in Mama's room or the moonlight coming through the window over my desk or the sound of the dogs barking: Spud and Annie in the yard, and the other dogs—the pack—yelping and baying down at the barn. But I was awake and I looked at my clock—4 in the morning— and knew that dogs were in the sheep.

While I was grabbing the sweater and jacket I had left piled on the chair in front of my desk, I heard the "click-click-click" of cartridges as Mama dropped them into the tube beneath the barrel of the .22. I didn't have to see her check the breech or yank the stock hard toward her to force back the hammer because I knew how she did it and never wasted time doing it and never hurried or got careless.

With guns you don't hurry, she would say.

Do what you have to do; do it right; don't hurry.

When I walked into her room she was pulling on a sweater. Normally she would have worn a thick jacket and gloves, but not for this.

She just nodded toward the hall. I went on outside, with her right behind.

It was perfectly clear. Cold, but not like you imagine winter. Snowmelt was already beginning to drip from the roof into the washtub we have on the concrete porch. A full white moon hung low in the sky, just above the barn.

We walked fast, boots crunching in the snow.

"I didn't close the gate," she said.

"Why not?"

"The lamb. The lamb that got stuck."

And I remembered.

"We didn't think about it then, of course. And no one could have known that the snow would stop so soon or that the sky would clear or even that there would be a full moon at all.

A moon that makes dogs go in packs.

It was so clear that you could see across the pasture as though it were day. There were five dogs. Two of them—one big and yellow, another just ankle high, black and white—were tearing at a ewe, ripping her while she lay trying to get up. The black and white dog had her leg, and the big one's fangs had dug in just behind her throat. He kept tugging at her and pulling her across the snow. She would fall, struggle, rear her head, and fall again, with the black and white dog growling and darting behind her.

The other dogs had already killed four sheep that lay like bags of bloodmeat and wool, in a line toward the creek.

In the lot, the rest of the sheep stood perfectly still, bleating but not moving.

"All right," Mama said. "Get down."

I dropped to my elbows and knees. It was very important to be still.

"Ready?"

"I'm ready."

She lay on her stomach behind me and laid the rifle barrel across my back.

Be a rock. Don't move. The gun is resting on a solid rock. And I knew what she was thinking. Squeeze the trigger. Squeeeze. Be still. Be careful. Take your time. Squeeeze.

Crack.

I can't describe the sound a bullet makes when it hits an animal. I can't even try. The sound makes you sick, even if the animal has to be shot. Even if it deserves to be shot. I can't describe either how the animal jumps and yelps and whips around, thrashing, biting itself, trying to tear the wound out with its teeth.

All the other dogs took off running toward the creek. The yellow dog kept throwing itself into the snow and crying in machine gun quick yelp-screams.

"All right. Again."

I tucked my head between my hands and waited.

Crack.

A cloud of snow flew up beside the dog that had now dragged itself behind the ewe.

"Damn."

The dog somehow managed to get up and start running, dragging one leg.

"You want to shoot again."

"No. I know where to find him."

By the time she got through the gate and into the pasture all the dogs were gone.

She went first to the ewe that the yellow dog had been attacking. Something made me watch while she jerked the rifle stock back, stood straight and pointed the barrel down so its tip was only an inch or two above the ewe's eye.

But I knew enough to look away before she pulled the trigger.

She had to go to all four sheep. Twice there were shots. Two other times, though, you could see that the pile that had been a ewe was too big, that the sheep's insides had already been pulled out of it. Then there was no need for gunshots.

I had started crying before she got back.

That was dumb. It wouldn't help anything.

You needed to be like Mama.

You just needed to do what had to be done.

Her pants, when she came back through the gate, were soaked in blood and there were patches of blood on her forehead.

Instead of wiping her own face, though, she gave her handkerchief to me.

"Here. Wipe your eyes."

"Sorry."

Sometimes you can't get your breath when you're crying. It's like hiccupping, but it isn't funny.

"I just . . . can't stop."

"It's OK. You're OK," she said. "Now come on."

We started back toward the house. There was a strip of rose light in the east; the sun was coming up.

"I want you to get some dry clothes on when we get home, Katie. Then make some coffee. Can you do that?"

"Sure."

"You did good."

"I don't know, it's just . . . I don't . . ."

"It'll be all right. It goes with raising sheep."

When we got home, I got out the coffee pot. Mama washed her face, put on another pair of pants, took the rifle and opened the back door.

"I'll be ten minutes."

"You want me to make something else?"

"If you want to."

"You going after the dog?"

She nodded, then closed the door.

I slipped some bacon slices into the skillet, turned the heat on, and listened as the pop and sizzle mixed with the splashing of snow water on the porch outside. The sun had come up; the sky was clear. Looking across beyond the orchard, you could see buzzards circling the pasture.

It took ten minutes for the bacon to fry; I was just taking it up when Mama got back. She had the gun with her when she walked through the kitchen.

"Did you get him?"

"Yes, I got him. Tell you what—why don't you go down and feed the chickens while I clean the rifle. Then we'll scramble eggs and make the rest of breakfast."

"Bacon'll be cold."

"That's all right. I want to get this behind us. What about school?"

"I don't know."

"Turn on the radio."

"I just forgot."

"I know. Tough morning."

The radio sat on the drain board, under the window. I could hear the announcer from the Waxahachie station as I walked down the hall toward my room.

"Stay right here. We'll keep you up to date on the school closings we have so far. The forecast is clear and warmer today with snow melting—still we have a number of schools that will be closed today. Red Oak Schools, Milford Schools, Ferris Schools, Waxahachie Schools, Ovilla Schools, Midlothian Schools, Ennis Schools, Palmer Schools . . ."

And he went on.

All we cared about was Midlothian.

She looked up when I came back into the kitchen. She had a rod and some white cotton pads. She put a drop of oil on each of the pads and then ran them several times through the gun barrel.

"Did you hear the radio, Katie?"

"Yes."

"Probably a good thing. You can get some of the sleep you missed. Go on and feed the chickens—after we eat breakfast you can go back to bed."

"Don't you have to bury the sheep?"

"I can do that by myself."

"I want to help."

"We'll see."

I nodded and went outside.

I was halfway to the chicken house when the red truck turned in our driveway. It pulled up in front of me. The hog-jowled driver leaned across the cab.

"Your mother at home?"

"Yes, sir."

He nodded, heaved himself up under the steering wheel, gunned the engine until the tires caught traction, and swerved the truck up toward the house.

I followed.

I was just even with the garage when Mama came out of the back door.

He got out of his truck and walked up to her. He put his hand on the back of his neck. He didn't seem to be talking that loud, but you could his rumble voice clear.

"That your truck?"

"Yes."

"You just been over to my place?"

"I have."

"Kill a dog there?"

"Your dog's a sheep killer."

"That dog ain't never killed nothing in his life."

"Until this morning."

"You're wrong about that. That's a house dog. That dog plays with my kids. I got kids crying now."

"I have sheep dead."

"Not from my dog."

She didn't answer but just took off her glasses and wiped them with the handkerchief she carried in her back pocket. Then she turned and came toward the truck which was ten feet from where I was standing. She leaned over the bed, fixed her feet on the ground, and heaved. Over the tailgate slid the dead dog, yellow and blood-soaked, its body thudded on the snow like a sack of feed.

Then she drug the dog across the yard and let it fall at the man's feet.

He stared down at it.

She pulled a stick out of her jacket pocket, rammed it between the dog's jaws, and twisted. Blood poured out of the mouth.

Then she got down on her knees and started picking wool from between the teeth.

The wool wasn't just between the teeth—it was all over the inside of the mouth. She reached in with her thumb and forefinger and got whole bloody tufts out and spread them on the top of the gas meter beside her.

After the top of the meter was covered with the mess, she looked up.

"That enough?"

He nodded.

"You better go," she said. "Take your dog."

23

"I guess you want to talk money."

She just shook her head, got to her feet, threw the stick down and walked inside.

I followed her, turning my head once to watch as the man threw the dog's body into the bed of his truck.

Inside, we listened to the truck drive away.

"Let's go bury the sheep," she said.

The thing I'll remember about how we found them in the pasture—the buzzards had been at them first, of course—was the smoke rising from a melted circle of snow around each body, as though pipes for steam had been buried under the ground.

Mama looked at the bodies lined across the pasture and said, "Old poem— 'Three smiles that are worse than grief: the smile of a wolf about to spring; the smile of your lover who has betrayed you; the smile of melting snow.'"

We took the sheep carcasses to a waterway on the northwest side of the farm. It took most of the morning to bury them.

That afternoon I stayed in my room, looking out the window and thinking about the smile of melting snow.

Always,

Katie Haw

Calf Fries

Calf Fries

March 19, 1967
Midlothian, Texas

Dear Katie Dee,

It was a March day when R.C. Barnes—I found out later it stood for Robert Chambers Barnes but I didn't know that then and thought it was like Pepsi and R.C., and I always wanted an R.C. Cola to drink when I thought of his name—but it was a March day when he came out from the ASCS office in Waxahachie and wanted to measure our wheat. The wind had been blowing for a week. March in Texas is harsh; there are these little wisps of clouds way up in the sky, higher even than the highest jet planes fly.

Planting the wheat had not been easy, Katie Dee. You do it with a drill, but not a drill like the dentist uses. The drill we have, you pull behind the tractor. It's just a big long metal box. That's where the wheat seed goes. Under the box are eight holes, and under those holes eight long metal tubes leading down to the ground. The tubes go down between the metal discs of the planter—or really drill, like they call it in Texas, I don't see why, because seed gets planted but nothing really gets drilled.

The problem is, sometimes the holes in the bottom of the metal box get stopped up with too much seed, and nothing goes down through them. If that were to happen, and you wouldn't catch it, then you would have a bare strip in the field where no seed got in the ground. So the people who made the drill put in

27

a little hole just beneath the box, and they put a seat on the back of the drill. You can sit on the seat and see the stream of seed falling down through the metal tube. If whoever's sitting on the seat hollers out 'Stop!' then the tractor driver knows that the drill's gummed up again and stops.

You might think that Mama would drive the tractor and I would get to sit on the seat behind the drill.

But that wouldn't be Mama.

We had just been to Ovilla and filled the five gallon gas can. She was pouring gas in the tank of the tractor, which was out north of the garage, and I was buttoning my heaviest jacket. The wind, out of the north, whistled around the eaves of the garage, and you could hear loose shingles on the garage rattling.

"You drive the tractor."

"What?"

"Drive the tractor."

"I can't drive the tractor."

"You have to learn. You're almost five feet tall and that means your feet can reach the clutch and the brake."

"But I can't drive anything!"

"You don't get to be a kid forever."

"Why can't I sit on the drill seat and watch the wheat?"

"Because that's what I'm going to do."

"No fair!"

"I have papers to grade."

"What! You can't grade papers and watch the wheat too!"

"I can do anything while grading papers. I can grade papers and eat. It doesn't matter. Trust me. The wheat will be watched."

"So, why don't I get to sit on the drill and do my homework?"

"Let's go. Time to plant."

And that's what we did. Actually we changed jobs every now and then. I would drive for a while, and then she would drive. It's not as hard as you would think. The accelerator is a little lever by your hand. You pull it back as far as it will go and you don't touch it again until you're ready to stop. You have to push in the clutch, which means sticking your left leg way down—and then you put the gearshift in third—that's the gear you run the planter in—then you let out the clutch real slow, but the tractor still kind of lurches and jumps and she almost falls off the drill seat and screams but you can't hear her because the tractor's roaring and the wind is roaring and the dirt is blowing and then you let the clutch out all the way and you're off!

We planted for ten hours a day on Monday and Tuesday—it was spring break at school and so I was out, poor me—and every now and then I remember looking back, to see her sitting there with a fur cap and bluejean jacket, holding on to her blue notebook that had papers clamped down so they wouldn't blow away.

It rained Wednesday. Perfect timing.

And then, I remember, it was Friday morning. We were going to take lambs to Fort Worth the next day. I happened to look out my bedroom window, and the grain was just shining there, green grass except you knew it would be wheat some day, between the terraces that led up the hill to the east. We walked out into it, kind of congratulating ourselves and, I guess, God, and every now and then, each blaming the other when we came to a little bare strip (which, there weren't many of them, I have to say).

"Look, Mama. Long strip here, no wheat. That must have been while you were grading."

"Was not."

"Were too."

"Was not."

And like that.

And that afternoon R.C. Barnes had come out to see if we had overplanted. Normally, he told us, they didn't measure that soon after the grain was up. But we were one of the first crops in the county, and, since it *was* up, why not go ahead and get it measured.

I was proud that ours was one of the first crops in the county. He came that afternoon. His truck crunched up the gravel driveway and we went out to meet him. I didn't really know what an ASCS office was then, but I remember wondering about what he was doing when I saw all the big maps in the bed of his truck, and the chain and stakes.

"Mrs. Hawkins?"

"Yes?"

"I'm R.C. Barnes."

"I remember you from school. Measuring now?"

"Yes, ma'am, if that's all right."

"It's all right if you don't tell us we have to plow up anything."

He grinned. R.C. Barnes was a very tall man, with big combat boots that laced up past his ankles, and a maroon baseball cap that said 'A&M'.

"I won't tell you that you have to plow up anything."

"That a promise?"

"Yes, ma'am. The office will send you a letter in a few days. You won't know where to find me."

"Oh great. That's a pretty cowardly way of doing it, isn't it?"

"You bet."

He smiled again. He was getting his maps and contracts out of the truckbed, and I could tell that Mama liked him. She didn't smile, of course. She never smiles, except maybe once or twice a year—but she kept brushing the little blonde band of hair out of her eyes that always blows into her eyes but that mostly she doesn't care if it's there or not, and if she does care, and keeps brushing it back, then she likes you.

"No, Mrs. Hawkins, they can pay me to measure land, but there's not enough money on earth to make me tell a farmer to plow something up."

"I was going to sic the dogs on you."

She pointed to Spud and Annie, who, at this time in the afternoon, were up by the house asleep. Annie was just normal asleep, like a black rag the way she gets. Spud was kind of ridiculous asleep, hound dog asleep, lying on his back so that his ears lay on the ground beside him like dead leaves and flies were getting out of the wind on his whitepink stomach.

"Look like pretty rough dogs."

"You don't want to mess with them. They wake up mean."

"When?"

"About six o'clock this evening."

"I'm supposed to be in Ennis by then."

"Good thing for you."

"Mrs. Hawkins, I need a chain man. I don't suppose you could recommend anybody?"

"What do you pay?"

"I shortchain every measurement at least a rod."

"Take Katie."

"I was kind of hoping you would say that."

And of course I realized then that they were talking about me, and I smiled that stupid smile you have to smile when grownups talk about you and not to you. I had just come from chapter four of *The Mystery of the Spanish Cave*, which has a real dinosaur in it. I had some "buster" cookies, big marshmallow globs covered in chocolate, and was lying in my room listening to the wind howl, and the last thing I wanted to do was go out into the field with this man that I didn't even know, and really didn't understand what he was there for.

But sometimes you don't have a choice.

So, soon we were in his truck, bouncing up toward the back of the farm, where the first strip of wheat was coming up.

"So your mama doesn't like people from the government?"

"No, sir."

See, I figured this was Mama's fault. I had worked hard getting the wheat planted, and I wanted to have a day to relax in my room. There's just something about a holiday Friday in your room, when it's as sunshiney as summer outside but cold as winter and you can't get out of the wind.

So I didn't want to be 'nice.' I didn't want to lie, understand, but I didn't want to be 'nice,' either.

"No, she doesn't really like any people from the government."

"Why not?"

"Well, she says a long time ago people could make a living off the land. Now, she says, people still do that. Except a long time ago the people who made money were farmers. Now the people who make money are chemical salesmen, and tractor salesmen, and combine salesmen, and, especially, she says, county agents and agricultural extension agents, and a lot of other people who work for the government."

"They don't make a lot of money, though."

"Mama still hates them."

He laughed.

"She probably has a point."

We were going around the point of the middle waterway; he could see to the back of the farm now, where the steepest terraces were that we had planted.

He stopped the truck beneath a bodark tree at the end of the pasture fenceline. Then we both got out. He took one of the maps from the back of the truck. It had a stiff pasteboard back on it, and was about two and a half feet square. It was gray/black with all kinds of rectangles and squiggles on it.

"Well," he said, "that's not too good."

"What?"

"I bet these terraces aren't too old, are they?"

"I don't know."

"They sure aren't older than nineteen fifty eight, which is when this map was made."

"Is that bad?"

"Means we have to plot them in."

"How do we do that?"

He shook his head, took off his A&M cap, and ran a hand over his crew cut. He was very tanned. I guess he looked kind of handsome, in a kind of Gary Cooper way, except he wasn't as old as Gary Cooper, except that Mama says she doesn't like Gary Cooper.

"Come on. Let's sit by the fence. I'll show you about measuring."

We sat down so that both of us could see up the hill, following the terrace lines. Our backs were against the raspy bark of the tree. The other trees at the back of the pasture broke the north wind a little, but it was still cold.

"Got you a pretty good stand."

"Yeah."

"You help?"

"I drove."

"No kidding."

"It's not as hard as it looks."

"What did your mother do?"

"Sat on the drill. Graded papers."

"She's a teacher?" And that's when I guess I got a little mean. Like, that stupid I'm not. Part, he was trying to teach me how to measure land. Part, and probably a big part, he was trying to find out about Mama. And if he had just come out and said so, all right. But this way—I didn't not like him, you know? But I didn't want to make it easy for him.

"She's a professor," I said. I knew that would worry him.

"Professor of what?"

"Comparative Literature."

"What is that?"

"It's when you have to know lots of languages, and stuff like that."

He just kind of nodded. Probably he did not know lots of languages.

"All right, Katie Hawkins. Take a look at this map." I did. "This—this little square—is your farm, from two thousand feet."

"That?"

"That. See—there's the little square where your yard is. Here's the waterway, running up here. Here's where we are."

"Oh. There's the back fence."

"Yes. You got it. Now all up in there, is where your wheat is. You see the terraces on the map? See the curving lines?"

"No."

"That's because they aren't there. When the airplane took these pictures, the field was flat. The Soil Conservation Service must have terraced the farm in the late fifties. So we have to draw the terraces in."

"How do we do that?"

"Look. Do you see that pasture fence about a half mile distant?"

"It's Mr. Hall's east fence."

"There. See it on the map?"

"That line?"

"That line."

"I see it."

"Okay. If we walk this way—come on—right over here. . ."
I followed him.

"Now. We're right in line with that fence, you see that?"

"I see it."

"If the fence were extended, it would run right between our legs."

"I don't think I would like that."

"Me neither. But look. I'm going to put my ruler down on the map, and I'm going to extend it right down the Hall's fence, to this pasture. Now, I'm going to draw a line right down the ruler. If we walk straight toward that fence, not going right or left, keeping the old imaginary barbed wire right between our legs—we'll be walking up this line I've drawn on the map."

"I see that."

"Except I've got a special ruler. These little marks are chains."

"What's a chain?"

"This thing."

It looked more like a tape measure to me. A very long one. We kind of worked together on the chaining. A chain is twenty two yards long. He taught me how to step exactly twenty two yards, so I would know I was coming to the end of the chain.

We had drawn in two terraces when we took a break to drink some iced tea that he had in a cooler. By that time we were down by the stock pond. I took off my shoes and let them float in the water. He got a cigarette out of the pocket of his khaki shirt.

"How long have y'all farmed this place?"

"Three years."

"You buy it?"

"No. It's kind of been in the family. Mama grew up on it."

"But you weren't born here?"

"No. I was born in Atlanta. My dad was a pilot at Dobbins Air Force Base."

"I see."

"He flew F-4's. But then he was sent to Viet Nam and—you know."

"Yeah. That's tough."

"We're kind of over it now. I guess." He nodded. We didn't say anything for a while. I had to admit it, I kind of liked the way he was teaching me about measuring land. I could have made things harder for him. But if Mama had to go out with somebody, there could be worse.

"Isn't it kind of tough working the farm, just you two?"

"Mama knows a lot."

"She must. The place looks good."

"She knows a lot about farming. And raising sheep."

"She does this and teaches?"

"She just teaches part time."

"Where?"

"A lot of junior colleges."

"She doesn't want a regular teaching job?"

"I guess, but she can't get one."

"Why?"

"She gets fired a lot. She's always yelling at Deans, and stuff like that." That made him laugh a little.

"Farmers don't always make good college professors," he said.

"I wonder why," I said.

"Farmers are ornery," he said.

"Yeah, that's Mama," I said.

And then we went back to measuring.

We finished about five in the afternoon, and he took me back to the house. Mama asked him to come inside for a cup of coffee, like I kind of figured she might, although I don't know why I figured that, because she never asks anybody to come in for a cup of coffee, but I just kind of figured this time she might. So I stayed outside and played ball against the chimney.

I did that until about six, when I could smell that supper was almost ready.

There's something really good about supper in cold weather. It's almost dark, and the sky is dirty purple; there's a cold wind so that you have to wear your hood sweatshirt—and you can see the light in the living room window and the light in the kitchen window, and you can smell pork chops frying.

Mr. Barnes' truck was still in the driveway.

I hadn't been too surprised about the coffee. I was *very* surprised about supper.

That *never* happens.

We ate around the table in the kitchen. It was strange having someone else there. Mr. Barnes was so big, and his legs were so long, he almost didn't fit. His knees kept bumping against the under side of the table, and the whole table would shake when he cut his pork chops.

I've forgotten what they talked about; it seemed kind of boring.

So, pretty soon, I excused myself and went back to my room to kind of wonder about what was going on.

Because, of course, it had to go on sometime.

I remember in Atlanta when Mama and Daddy and I lived near Clairmont Park.

Those were good times, weren't they?

When we used to go to the Fernbank Science Center and walk through the nature trails?

Sometimes—I was just seven then—I would get up Saturday

mornings real early, and Daddy wouldn't have to fly that day. And I didn't mean to see through the door of where Mama and Daddy would be sleeping, but, you're getting cereal, and you don't want to bother them, and—you know. They'd just be lying there, Mama with her hair all tangled on the pillow, the whole room rumpled up and in that kind of light it is only on Saturday mornings—and every now and then you could hear Daddy talking real low, or Mama laughing the way she does.

And hasn't for a long time.

So I didn't really mind.

The wind was picking up. It sounded like coyotes, and made the house creak. It came through the windows on the north and east side of my room; outside you could see a half moon coming and going as clouds scudded in front of it, moving fast as witches. I felt like Halloween, turned on my reading light, got another blanket from the chest—we called it the 'possum' chest now, because the possum I wrote you about had bounced off it—and kind of burrowed in bed. It was only 7:30, but dark because it was purple wind world anyway, a good world to sleep in. I was halfway through with *The Mystery of the Spanish Cave.*

I finished it two hours later.

Mama and Mr. Barnes—I knew I could never call him 'Bob'— were in the living room, where they had been for it seemed like a long time. You could hear ice in glasses. Then it would be quietquietquiet and LOUDLOUDLOUDLAUGHLAUGH-LAUGH.

Finally I dozed off; I got up after midnight.

It was quiet except for the wind.

The door between my room and Mama's bedroom was closed. It had been open when I went to sleep.

I knew I shouldn't do it.

But I got out of bed. It was so cold. The floor was like you were walking across the inside racks of a refrigerator.

I tiptoed across the room. The rug felt warm on the bottoms of my bare feet.

When I got to the side of the bed I could look over it. Mama was lying there, wrapped like a caterpillar in cocoon blankets, her hair all blondrag spreadout. Her eyes opened, and she reached out for me.

"Honey?"

"Yes, Mama," I whispered.

"Did you have a nightmare?"

I thought about that one for a while.

"Yes," I answered, finally. "I don't know why it was a nightmare. But it was."

Then she grabbed me and pulled me down to her.

She was really warm.

"You silly thing. Silly bear."

"Yeah."

"Silly little bear."

Then I got up and went back to my room.

We got up at four o'clock the next day. You have to do that if you want to get to the stockyards when the buyers are making the rounds of the lamb pens. We didn't say much over breakfast. I noticed in the living room that there were two empty wine bottles. One of them must have been almost empty when Mama and Mr. Barnes started talking, because I don't think anybody could drink two whole bottles of wine.

At that time it was still dark, of course, and cold. It had cleared up during the night. The wind had died. The stars were as bright as you could imagine, but a sheet of ice had frozen over the lambs' water when we got to the barn.

She backed the truck down off the gravel road and into the

pasture while I put out ground corn for the lambs. They all thundered across the lot, the ewes knowing they couldn't get through the slats and into the stall; and while the lambs went desperate with the food, we opened the tailgate and made sure the sideboards were on right.

"OK, let's go."

It's hard work. You grab a lamb by its hind leg and jerk him away from the trough. Then you have to drag him to the slat wall and lift him over to the other person who's standing by the truck. The lamb is struggling all the time and wrestling—and of course I'm not strong enough to lift him over. Mama has to bend down from outside the stall and fasten onto a handful of backwool, and then the two of us together kind of haul him over like a sack of live cement. The lambs are supposed to weigh about eighty pounds, but Mama is strong enough to lift one up and slide it into the truck, between the tailgate and the sideboard.

We loaded ten of them. By the time we did that, there was a little gray in the east, and both of us were sweating. There wasn't any time to rest, though.

Mama hardly talked going up to Fort Worth. Just, 'Are you warm enough?' and 'Do you want the heater up higher?' and stuff like that. On the way north from the farm we didn't meet anybody, since it was just a little after five o'clock. Outside of Midlothian though, before you get on the Mansfield highway, you come to the edge of a plateau; and out on that edge the whole world opens up. Fort Worth to the northwest, and Cleburne to the south, and the lights of Grand Prairie and Arlington lining the horizon to the north, just like a painting that someone had made circling the windshield of your truck; and, all the time, the pink and yellow and green and blue that is morning, all coming up over Midlothian.

"What do you think we'll get?

"The morning paper said twenty seven a pound."

"That's pretty good, isn't it?"

"Yeah. If we get it."

"You think we will?"

"Never know. Depends on the commission man."

We went past downtown Fort Worth and then got on Northside Boulevard. On the right was The Northside Coliseum, with its big 'WRESTLING TONIGHT!' neon sign, and underneath that the posters of Duke Keomuka and Irish Danny Flannigan. Everybody on the streets had on cowboy hats. There were other trucks, some pickups like ours, but mostly big cattle carriers. The streets were not asphalt or concrete, but red bricks, and, to either side, you saw alleyways and pens and auction barns.

And you smelled what you only smell when you get around a whole lot of cattle and sheep and goats and pigs.

When we parked over behind the sheep pens the sun had just come up over Swift's Packing Plant. It was still cold out, but I had taken so much exercise I didn't mind.

Everywhere people yelled and ran and shouted. Stall men yelled at commission men; goats, bells tinkling around their necks, drove sheep into the inspection ramps, cows crowded down the cobblestone paths that led under the covered auction sheds—and pigs, as loud as you can imagine, from somewhere, so that you could hear it all over Fort Worth—just squealed.

"Here's a slot! Over here! Bring the green truck over here!" Mama worked the truck back, and the pen man held up his hand when we were at the gate. Then we could hear the side board being almost torn off its hinges and the sheep driven down the ramp, marked with blue chalk as they skidded down the board.

"Name?"

41

"Hawkins!" she shouted back, while the man scribbled on some papers he had on a noteboard. Then, before she could get out of the truck, he ran up to the driver's door and held the lading notice out for her to sign.

"Commission man?"

"Myers."

"Right."

"What are they getting?"

The man just spit and shook his head:

"Ain't no way of knowing."

"All right. We'll check back."

Then she pulled the truck up and parked it a hundred yards or so from the pens.

"Let's go through the pens. We'll try to find Myers."

"Right."

You could climb a kind of catwalk that led between stalls about fifteen feet square. Each stall had gates on two sides, and groups of sheep marked with red, orange, and blue chalk depending on your commission man trampled into one area and out another. Buyers leaned on the top fence rails and pointed to this animal or that, and yelled, like everybody else was yelling. It was all under a huge tin roof about fifty feet up, so that the noise just bounced back down at you; while pen men worked their way through the flocks, opening this ewe's mouth to show how the teeth were, or examining udders, or checking hooves. The buyers just kept watching and spitting and taking off their hats to rub their hair, and then spitting again.

We had worked our way halfway back, through and around and over what seemed like a million pens and a zillion sheep, when Myers yelled at us.

"Mrs. Hawkins!"

"Yes! Did you see the lambs?"

"I saw them."

"What do you think?"

"I don't have to think. They look good."

"All right. We're going to go over to Cattleman's and have breakfast. You think you might have an offer by nine o'clock?"

"I know I won't have an offer by nine o'clock."

"Why not?"

"Because I have an offer right now."

"You're kidding."

"It's moving fast today. Man from Armour picked 'em up just after you unloaded."

"What have you got?"

"Twenty-eight and a half."

"Wow," I kind of yelled, because that was the most we had ever gotten.

Mr. Myers grinned down at me. He was a big man, with a stomach that always hung over his belt buckle a little. I had never seen him without khaki work clothes on, or the end of a cigar in his mouth; or, for that matter, without the same straw cowboy hat.

"You think that's an acceptable price, young lady?"

"I think so."

"What about you, Mrs. Hawkins?"

"You made our day."

"No, ma'am, I think Armour Star made your day."

"Whatever. We can afford breakfast now."

"You sure can. Here. You want to sign this contract?"

"Give it here."

She signed it, and just like that we had made two hundred dollars.

And were headed to Cattleman's.

We had to wind through the rest of the sheep barns and then

over to Merchant's Walk. This was the fun street at the stockyards, because you could read the signs. Boots and Stetson's. Leddy's, Home of the World's Finest Custom Saddles. The Exchange, Fort Worth's Finest Hotel.

And of course, The Cattleman's Steak House.

It was always dark when you went in. But all around the walls you saw pictures of these huge cows. Or bulls. Or steers. I don't know which is which between bulls and steers, but I think bulls are the ones without the horns and steers are the ones with their heads up over the doorway, maybe six feet from horn tip to horn tip and you wonder how anybody ever got close enough to that steer to touch its head in the first place, let alone stuff it.

I always walked around and looked at the pictures. Mostly they were paintings of huge, red/brown fat chunks of cattle, their stomachs almost touching the ground. Under each painting some words would have been written:

Grand Champion Polled Hereford
Fort Worth Fat Stock Show
1939: Sold to Cattleman's Steak House

There were maybe thirty of them, from all across the country, but mostly from Fort Worth; and up at the front, there was the showcase where they had steaks of every cut and size you could think of, lying in the middle of chunks of ice, with a man standing behind them turning slabs of meat on a grill that fired up and steamed and charred so that he would sprinkle it with just a touch of water and then turn the steaks and bellow the fire again, the waitresses lining up to take meat away as fast as he could get it ready.

And big waitresses.

These weren't teenage girls, like you sometimes saw at the

Dairy Queen in Midlothian. All of these women were bigger than Mama, maybe not taller, but bigger through the middle and with more muscles in their arms and wrists and hair so high and twisted and pinned and brooched that they had to have strong shoulders and necks just to hold their own hair up, much less the huge platters of meat and baked potatoes if you came at night, or breakfast steaks and grits and toast and eggs and biscuits and bacon and sausage if you came mornings.

We sat toward the back. Around us were hardwrinkled men and women, drinking coffee, with giant plates of food or used-to-be-food-and-is-now-tobacco-ashes, covering the tables in front of them. And of course the men kept their Stetson hats on all the time because, according to Mama, west of Cleburne it's not polite to take off your hat inside.

Above us, looking very peaceful and fat and heavy in a green pasture with blue skies, was the Black Angus that had won the Grand Exposition in St. Louis, Missouri, in 1947.

The waitress was there as soon as we sat down.

"Y'all want some coffee?"

"I do," said Mama.

"Coke for me."

"Large coke, Sugar?"

They always called you 'sugar' or 'honey.' Of course that's what they called the grown up women customers, too, or the grown up men customers. In fact they called everybody 'sugar' or 'honey', so I didn't mind it.

"Yes, ma'am, large coke."

"I'll have that for you in a minute."

Mama and I looked at the menu while she was gone. On the top of the menu were written the words: "Calf Fries Our Specialty."

"What do you want, Katie?"

"I don't know."

"You hungry?"

"I'm starved."

"Well, what looks good?"

"I don't know. All this stuff. What's 'calf-fries?'"

"Oh. Calf fries are great. Try some. You come to Fort Worth, you got to try calf fries."

"What are they?"

"Just another cut of meat. Breaded and fried."

"What comes with them?"

"Hash browns, probably."

"OK, I'll try those."

So I ordered calf fries when the waitress came back. Mama read the newspaper until the food came.

It came in giant platters, so that the waitress had to clear off the salt and pepper shakers, and move the water glasses, and rearrange the silverware. Then down her arm slid the grits—in a separate dish—and the toast, and the biscuits, and the scrambled eggs, and the breakfast steak Mama had ordered, and the hash browns, and, with a plate of ketchup on the side, my calf fries.

"Try 'em."

"OK."

I cut them with a knife, but they were tender enough to eat with a fork.

"Put butter on them."

"What about this ketchup?"

"Yep. Ketchup too. They're a specialty."

They weren't bad, and especially they weren't bad because I was starving.

"Taste a little like something; I'm not sure what it is, but like something I've had before."

"Seafood?"

"Right. Maybe seafood."

"Oysters?"

"Right again, Mama. They're a little like oysters."

"They're good for you like oysters, too."

It was then I noticed a man at another table, watching me. His face looked like it had been baked on him with dark brown modeling clay, which somebody had then scratched all over with a hay rake.

"She likes them calf fries, does she?"

"Looks like it," Mama said.

The man took out a cigarette, lit it, and blew smoke up toward whichever prize Hereford was standing above the dark wood by his table.

"That's the best food they is, calf fries."

"I always thought so," said Mama.

The man stood up then. He almost bumped on the chandelier, but he didn't because he bent down a little. He was one of those men who bent down a lot, because ceilings and doors and things were always too short for him. He had a belt buckle as big as our mailbox; he hooked his hands on it and hung his claywrinkled face over our table:

"You go on eatin' those, young lady, you'll amount to something. Brain food."

After a while the man left. I went on eating the calf fries, which Mama seemed to think was funny and now I know why, but I didn't then.

"So what," she asked while I was draining the last of the ketchup and getting ready to ask for more, "was this nightmare that you had last night?"

"Nothing. Just a dream."

"Just a dream about what?"

"Nothing."

"Had to be something. I woke up and there you were. I thought you were a ghost."

"I don't know."

"You don't sleepwalk."

"No."

"So what was it, anyway?"

"I just—wanted to kind of check on you."

"Check on me for what?"

"I don't know."

"You weren't worried, were you?"

"Why would I be worried?"

"I don't know. Why would you?"

I just shook my head.

"It's just—you and Mr. Barnes were having such a good time. I thought…"

"Oh."

"I mean, it would have been all right."

"You think so?"

"Sure." She laughed. "Bob Barnes and I are old friends."

"You knew him before?"

"Sure. Went to high school with him."

"Oh. Did you go out with him?"

"Nah. I didn't out in high school. Just studied all the time."

"That must have been awful."

"Pretty boring."

"When did you… I mean…"

"Discover boys?"

"Yeah."

"I never discovered boys. In college I discovered men."

"There's a difference, huh?"

"There's a difference."

"And Daddy was different, huh?"

"Yes, darling. Daddy was different."

Then I was quiet for a time.

So was she.

"Mama, I... I mean, it would be all right with me, if you..."

"If I what?"

"You know."

"No. What?"

"If you wanted to date somebody."

She laughed.

"Kids 'date,' Katie. People my age 'have relationships.'"

"What's the difference?"

"Dating is fun."

"Oh. But it would still be all right."

She shook her head.

"I don't think we're quite ready for that."

"What do you mean?"

"I don't know. We've got dogs. We've got sheep. We're just not set up to take care of a man. We don't have the facilities."

"I guess not."

"Maybe someday."

"Yeah," I said, agreeing with her, but figuring it wouldn't be soon, because when Mama talks about Daddy she—I don't know. You just know, it won't be soon.

Anyway, we did a lot of stuff after the meal. I mean, we had two hundred dollars, and it felt like a good day. We went to Leddy's, where I picked out a leather belt, and they put my name on it. We went past the coliseum, where they were getting ready for the night's rodeo. We walked over to the auction barn and heard the auctioneer, the way he speaks that language nobody's ever heard before and doesn't sound like anything but a cattle auctioneer, and I sat on the back row and was scared to move or blink an eye, thinking he might make a little gesture with his hand toward me, and I would have bought a cow.

Finally, about three in the afternoon, we drove home.

It was warm in the truck, and, between Mansfield and Venus, I fell asleep.

This time I didn't have any nightmares.

By the way, Mama told me later what calf fries are.

You don't want to know.

Katie Haw

Mayfate

Mayfate

May 7, 1967
Midlothian, Texas

Dear Katie Dee,

They say that storms always come on the day of the Mayfate. Since this was my first Mayfate, Katie Dee, I don't know. But we had been having crazy weather all week, and Friday was worse. There was a big thunderstorm at about two in the afternoon during math class. The people who sat next to the big wall of windows along the north side of the building got pretty nervous when it darkened up outside and rain pelted down like somebody had turned a hose on the school.

This was not necessary for me, you know? I mean, like, I really needed it? It was hard enough to deal with math when I was only thinking of whether my straps would fall down, or if the purse I was going to carry would really go with the light blue gown; or, worse, if Jeremy would be able to get close enough to me in the middle of the gym floor that I could give him my arm.

We had been practicing for a month, but I had been wearing jeans.

Tonight I was going to have on a formal gown that was big enough at the bottom to cover the circle with the panther in it in the middle of the gym floor.

What if he couldn't reach me?

All this to think about, and a scary thunderstorm, too.

But as it turned out, the storm had passed on by about five-thirty in the afternoon, and when we got to the high school and parked as close to the gym as possible—because there were a lot of cars, even that early—it was just puddle dripping and bright lateafternoon sun weather, May all the way, warm and muddy, with that band of thunderstorms flashing way off to the southeast.

"Oh no."

"Katie!"

So of course, like an idiot, I stepped out of the truck and into a little hole of standing water.

"Look out, Katie!"

"I'm sorry, I'm sorry! Oh look at these shoes!"

"Come here—here, sit on the side of the seat. I can dry them."

And she did, with a towel that she carried behind the truck seat. But I thought, is this the way the whole night is going to go?

I didn't want to make a fool of myself in front of the entire town.

Still, it was kind of exciting when we turned the corner around the high school building, me holding Mama's arm and still grating and slipping a little on the asphalt even though the high heels were only short ones—I'm better than I used to be but it's still hard—we turned that corner, and there, for a hundred yards or so on the blocked off street between the gym and the high school, was the whole royal party, from the first grade on up.

"Oh look at them! Aren't they cute?"

"They're not 'cute', Mama, they're the royal party."

"I know, but—look at the little ones!"

And the littlest ones did look kind of cute, I had to give her that. The dumb boys, throwing rocks and gravel at each other or jumping into lakes in the gravel while their mothers screamed at them, and combed their hair—and the girls, much more serious of course, fixing each other's gowns, and getting their lipstick just right.

It looked like a movie; boys all in black and white tuxedos, and girls in pink, or white, or blue: like Gone With The Wind, if all the actors were about as high as a yardstick.

After a while you could tell that everyone was headed toward the principal's office in the high school building. That was where pictures were being made. Actually pictures were being made everywhere, mostly by moms and dads, grandparents, whatever; but the official *Panther Scream* (that's the yearbook) photographer was set up in the principal's office. You were supposed to line up there beginning at six o'clock.

Mrs. Moore, who was very short and always dressed in black, paraded up and down in front of the trophy case, getting people lined up.

"Kindergarten Duke and Duchess! Florence Edwards and Timothy Gillespie! Where's—oh, there's Melanie. Melanie, where's Timothy? Timothy! There, you, Timothy! Come here and—will someone please comb Timothy's hair?"

We worked our way through a bunch of people at the door, and got into the corridor. I saw Jeremy about half way down the hall, leaning up against the third grade door, talking to a couple of fifth grade guys I don't know. Jeremy is such a Dufus, but he does make me laugh sometimes.

His mother kind of appeared out of nowhere then and grabbed me. She spun me around and held me out at arm's length, screaming at Mama:

"She is so *precious!* Oh Katherine, you are a *doll!* Nancy, this girl is a *doll!* Oh, look at your *hair*, Katie! The braid is just *darling!*

She went on like that for a while. She's a very big woman, and I couldn't get away from her. Mama smiled and talked to her, and pointed down the hall at Jeremy, and said that he looked very nice, too.

Which he did. Jeremy is a fox. A Dufus, but a fox.

"Dukes and Duchesses of the Fifth Grade!"

"Oh! Nancy, I believe they have to line up!"

"Yes, they do."

"You and Katie go on; I'll go get Jeremy!"

She tore off down the hall, her high heels clacking like a beagle's claws when the dog gets thrown on a tile floor and panics.

Mama put her arm around me while we walked to the end of the photo line.

"Katie?"

"Yes?"

"Don't marry Jeremy."

"All right."

"Not ever."

"I won't, Mama."

"Do you promise me?"

"I promise you."

"I'm not kidding about this, Katie, I'm not being facetious the way I sometimes am. If you marry him, even secretly, I'll track you both down and kill you before I have to be around that woman as an in-law."

"I won't marry him. Not even secretly. Jeremy is not really that bad, though. He's kind of funny."

"I don't want any more said about this."

"All right."

After a while Jeremy showed up at the end of the line. I wasn't but a little taller than him, and so we didn't have to have me sit on a stool and him stand behind me. That was not just chance, of course. I could have chosen Frog McKenzie, who is a lot

funnier than Jeremy, and no more of a pain—but then I would
have had to sit on the stool, which I do not want to do.

I don't like boys taller than me, but I don't want to be that
much taller than them, either.

It looks weird.

"Here's your corsage."

"Thank you."

"We didn't know what kind to get. So we got this."

"Thank you, Jeremy," Mama said, opening the box. "Oh yes,
this is a white chrysanthemum. Just perfect."

"Can you pin it on, Jeremy?" I asked, so it would make him
miserable.

He made motions with his arms and legs like he was in a
swimming pool, treading water; he kind of tried to take the
corsage back from Mama, but then it looked like he became
very sick, and couldn't touch it.

"I'll do it, Jeremy, if that's all right."

"Yes, ma'am, that would be fine."

She pulled my strap out a little, and pinned the corsage on.
As though it was that difficult. Ultimately Jeremy is going to
have to date a girl, and, somewhere along the line, I guess, touch
her.

If he doesn't wind up in a spastic ward first.

While we were in line waiting for the picture I couldn't talk
to Jeremy, who had nothing to say and just stood chewing his
gum, and it didn't feel comfortable talking to Mama about how
dumb Jeremy was, with him just standing there—so I remembered how I got elected, and how weird the whole thing was. It
was first period, geography. We were studying about Venezu-
ela, and what its basic principal products were—I forget what
they were, but I think soybeans, because soybeans are right for
a lot of principal products—and Mrs. Bergvall said we should

stop because it was time to vote for Duchess. So I wrote down Gretchen's name on a slip of paper and passed it in. She must have written mine down. Anyway *somebody* must have written mine down because, after Mrs. Bergvall had counted all the slips of paper, she announced that I was fifth grade Duchess, and everybody after school congratulated me.

When I got home on the school bus that afternoon—it was in late February—the wind was cold out of the north, and the fields still looked straw dead, and the sky was that pale blue that looks like it's been scraped clean. It was the cold that, you're supposed to be outside because it's sunny, but you're miserable still and you wish it would just snow and cloud over.

Mama was down at the tool shed with the tractor, taking off the busters, so that we could pull the drill to plant wheat. She had on her thick wool lined jacket, but nothing on her head. Her face and hands were covered with grease and oil spots.

"Mama!"

"What?" she asked, kind of disgusted. See, the busters are big plows, each sweep like metal angels' wings, two feet from tip to tip; they're heavy and hard to take off. Her knuckles bled— like they always do when she changes the plows, because, for some reason, she won't wear gloves. Says they get in her way. Anyway, she lay under the bar that extends out over and beyond the front tires, and everytime the lug wrench slipped she cussed, and banged the wrench on the sweep bar, and cussed and then cussed again.

"Mama!"

"Yes! Yes, what is it?"

"I got duchess."

"What?"

"I got duchess."

She slid out from under the tractor, wiped her forehead with

the back of her hand—which got more grease on her forehead—
and looked up at me. "I'm sure I didn't understand you."

"I got duchess." Then she kind of looked away, like she saw
something in the distance nobody else could see—she does that
a lot—and said, "An evening dress."

"What?"

"This means we have to buy an evening dress."

"Oh. By the way, I think Gretchen's mad."

"Why?"

"I think she wanted duchess."

"Oh."

"She wasn't unfriendly on the bus, but Robin Treadwell
walked out from school with me, and she said Gretchen was
really mad at me. I mean, she's been here since kindergarten
and never gotten duchess. I'm here three years and bang, I'm
it."

"Yeah. Life is tough."

"What it means is, I get to be in the Mayfate."

"May fete."

"What?"

"May fete. The fetes of May. Rites of spring. The community dances in celebration of fertility. The celebration of new
birth, all that. See, 'fete' is a celebration. A community celebration. 'Fate,' is something that's destined to happen. You understand?"

That's Mama's college teacher self, and when she gets like
that you have to just nod.

"You understand, Baby?"

"Yes. Anyway, I get to be in the Royal Party at the Mayfate.
I also have to choose a Duke. That's the yucchy part."

"Are there any boys that you like?"

"One or two, I guess."

"Don't choose them. Anybody else?"

"Jason. He's a fox."

"I think they require human beings, Dear."

"Mama..."

"All right. Who makes you laugh?"

"Todd. Jeremy."

"Choose one of them. If a man can't make you laugh, he isn't worth having around."

"Mama, were you ever in the Mayfate when you grew up here?"

"Yes. Everybody in Midlothian goes through the May Fete. No way around it."

"Were you a Duchess?"

"Yes, I was a Duchess."

"What grade?"

"Eighth."

"I'm a Duchess in the fifth grade."

"Go gather up the eggs."

And so now here I was, just about next in line to have my picture taken.

That went OK, although Jeremy's mom was never very happy about his hair and the way the cummerbund looked. The photographer seemed very tired; he was big and beefy with a sweat-through white shirt and had black, long hair that came over his forehead and that he kept having to kind of whoosh back by throwing his head back, the way a horse throws her tail. Every time he held up the little bulb he squeezed to make the picture he whooshed, and he whooshed at every joke he told to make people laugh—he told three, which he alternated so people standing next to each other wouldn't have to pretend to laugh at the same joke—and it whooshed every time he pulled the metal plate out from the tripod camera, smiled, and said, 'Next couple, please.'"

I'm *so* glad I didn't have to sit on the stool.

Francie Simmons is a *foot* taller than Barry Muller.

I have no idea why she chose him.

When the picture taking was over it was time to gather in the gym foyer. The street was still wet from the afternoon rain. A little white fingernail of a moon hung up in the west sky, with a bright star beside it, almost inside the curve of it. We might as well have been in a thunderstorm all over again, with all the flashbulbs going off in front of the gym.

"OK, girl. I'm going to get my seat. Good luck."

"All right."

She hugged me and said:

"I'm very proud of you, Duchess."

"Thanks, Mama."

Then she made her way into the gym.

It was seven fifteen now. A lot of the crowd had arrived. All the Duchesses were taken into the lunchroom, just to the side of the foyer. It was the same lunchroom I ate in every day; black and white tile floors, long tables, serving line in the back where you got fish sticks, spinach, weeners with ranch sauce, and navy beans—not all on the same day, of course—it was that lunch room, but it had never looked this way before. The Ladies in Waiting to Her Majesty stood by the south windows, adjusting each other's bows and patting each other's hair with very delicate palm touches.

Teachers in their best Sunday clothes—and I mean all of the teachers were there, Mrs. Moore, Mrs. Nelson, Mrs. Everett, Mrs. Falkner—one teacher almost for each child, all standing, looking at their watches.

From the music room on the other side of the foyer you could hear the trumpeters practicing scales and fanfares.

I just walked back and forth, breathing deep, being nervous. It was almost dark now. The last of the crowd was arriving. There were twenty rows of seats in the gym—not metal, shaky, rows of seats like you see in some new gyms, seats you can roll out like an accordian—but solid wood seats that had been there forever and seemed like the whole world could fit in. And even then, a lot of people had to stand on Mayfate night.

"All right!"

Mrs. Moore. She stood at the lunchroom door, her fingers held against her lips.

It became very quiet in the lunch room. Then came the trumpet notes:

The Grand March from the opera *Aida*.

Ta taaaa...tatata taaa taaa taaa...

"All right: Heralds, go!"

The two high school girls who were narrators—that's what a herald is—went out the door together then. You could hear them walking out in time with the music.

The loudspeaker squeaked and squealed and then settled down, probably because Mr. Caldwell tinkered with it.

Then the Heralds' first words:

"The Court of Her Majesty, the Queen of May. All rise."

You could just visualize everyone getting up. Then the trumpeter—just one of them—played The Star Spangled Banner.

Then:

"Ladies and Gentlemen. His Royal Majesty, The King of May. Jim, of the House of Day."

There he was, you could see him through the lunch room door, for just a few seconds, walking across the foyer, jumping up the steps, and going out into the gym. Jim Day. He was blond, and he had a scholarship to Texas A&M, to play tailback.

He was the tallest man in the high school.

"The Court of Her Majesty, The Queen of May. Duke and Duchess of the First Grade. Emily, of the House of Schmidt. Cody, of the House of Hitchcock."

And the line began to move forward, toward the door.

"Duke and Duchess of the Second Grade. Debbie, of the House of Hitchcock. Sam, of the House of Culpepper."

Finally it was time.

"All right, Katie. Come to the door."

There it was, all stretched out in front of me. The Mayfate. My first one ever. The gym ceiling, high up and arched and circled over us, its big rafters making diamond patterns that you could just see in the light of the film cameras. Then row after row of people, just shadows now, not moving, holding their breath it seemed like, stretching out from the goal we were under down as far as I could see to beyond the other goal; four pairs of Dukes and Duchesses started the semi-circle around the throne, standing, kind of fidgeting; and Jim Day, as tall as anybody I've ever seen standing right under the basket so that I thought his head might bump up against it, looking like the blond haired King of England, standing and waiting for me.

"Duke and Duchess of the Fifth Grade. Jeremy Allen, of the House of Spencer. Katherine Marie, of the House of Hawkins."

Ta Taaaaaa. Ta ta ta ta ta ta...

I started walking.

You could hear the cameras whirring, and the popping flash-bulbs almost blinded me. On the other side of the court Jeremy was only a moving shadow, staying, oh thank you God, right in the same place in the corner of my eye. It was all right. I knew we were even. We had practiced this too much not to be even. If he was there, in my left eye, we had to be right. No. Mrs. Moore yelling from the basketball scorer's platform, "Slow it down, Jeremy, wait for him Katie, move it on now, too fast, too slow—no, he was moving just right, and my high heels were wobbling a little but not so that anyone could tell.

Ta taaaa. Ta ta ta ta *ta ta*...

Halfway to center court.

Jim Day was looking straight at me. And then he smiled! He had been so stern before, as though I was doing something wrong—but then he gave the biggest smile, and, looking straight back at him, I smiled too. The King of May! Who, while I was in the end zone at the Ferris game playing keep away with the little rubber football, with a bunch of kids I barely even knew— who, just before halftime, took a kickoff from Ferris and came thundering toward us down the sideline, the whole orange and white world chasing blue and white him, and the whole Midlothian grandstand up and jumping and shaking the stands and roaring Go Sonny Go Sonny Go Sonny—because everybody called him 'Sonny'—who, was as much of a real King as I ever thought I would see and probably ever will see—he, Jim Day, smiled at me.

And then we were at the circle, the snarling panther under me, Jeremy crossing behind me now, my dress rustling on the floor, and, hold my right arm out now, palm on my chest, elbow sticking out as far as it can over that circle, come on Jeremy, come on Jeremy—yes! Linked up! And let's go!

We just glanced at each other once; he shook his head to get that lock of brown hair back out of his eyes. He was, and is, a dufus, and I'm much faster than he is, and he is a million miles from being Jim Day.

But he does make me laugh.

He makes me mad, too.

About a week after I chose him I was in the drug store. Mama had picked me up from school and gone to the hardware store and lumber yard. When she does that, I walk across the street to Hilley's Rexall Drug that has a blue and white sign with a line through the 'x' in Rexall—you've seen drug stores like that—well anyway I went to the back where they have three booths where teenagers usually sit but the back booth was free this time so I ordered a hamburger and a coke—Mama said I could because she was going to have to teach that night and dinner would just be a snack anyway—and, while they were making it, I went to the magazine rack behind the last booth and found the new "Uncle Scrooge." There is nothing more fun than that. You have a comic, which they let you take to the booth, and you're reading it waiting for the hamburger, which you can smell frying on the griddle halfway up the counter, beyond the other booths.

This time Uncle Scrooge wanted a golden coat—he's so greedy—and so he tried to find the golden fleece that Jason sailed after with the Argonauts.

But I was about halfway into the story, just where the Larkies swoop down on Donald and the kids, when the hamburger and Jeremy arrived at the same time. I hated it especially because the hamburger was so perfect. You know, the way a good drug-store makes a hamburger? The bun hot and glistening with grease, which just oozes through that waxey kind of paper they wrap it in, and onions and pickles sticking out of one side like the intestines out of a cut up pig—so Jeremy sits down with me!

I can't believe he did that!

I mean, that's OK in high school. But a boy and me in one booth in the drug store after school...

I was so embarrassed.

He wanted to talk about the Alamo, because we knew there was going to be an Alamo part to the Mayfate.

"Why didn't they just go around?" he asked, that brown shock of hair getting in his eyes like it always does.

And me, not believing that he is sitting there with the sleeve of his blue jean jacket getting in a mustard stain someone else has left on his side of the booth; and him, eating one of my french fries!

"Why didn't *who* just go around, Jeremy?"

"Santa Anna."

"What do you mean, 'why didn't he just go around?'"

"Well, he had, like, two thousand soldiers, didn't he?"

"He had about eighteen hundred, like it says in the Texas History book."

"Yeah, about that. Can I have some more of these?"

"Like I'm going to stop you?"

"Thanks."

"You're welcome."

"Well how many guys were in the Alamo?"

"One hundred and eighty six."

"So why did he have to stay there for so many days just to kill those guys? Why didn't he just leave them and go around the Alamo?"

I just shook my head.

"Honestly, Jeremy."

Boys.

Of course, now that I think back on it, I'm not so sure myself why Santa Anna just didn't go around, I will give Jeremy that much.

I asked Mama a couple of nights later. She said the Mayfate shouldn't do the Alamo because it was unfair to Hispanic Americans. Then she changed the subject.

So here I was, with this dufus, walking toward the King of May.

It seemed like forever. The farther we went, the more cameras there were—and now there are these huge lights, standing on poles, taller than a man. Their buzzing mixes with even more whirring cameras as every man in Midlothian is kneeling on the sidelines squinting through a camera with a white-hot glowing flash.

We are in front of the throne.

Jeremy bows... Jim Day nods... I kneel, look down, and rise. He nods.

Then we go left, past the first graders... past Emily Donald and Jason Waters of the third grade... and now in front of the metal chairs we will sit on.

Both of us kind of go "Whew," and we smile at each other.

It takes fifteen minutes for the rest of the royal party to come in. But then there we all are, waiting, gown-tuxedo, gown-tuxedo, bow-and-ruffle white blue yellow pink huge flowing lace flower kids, waiting for the Queen of the May.

"ALL RISE!"

Echo. Squeal of microphone, echo. ALL RISE all rise all ri..

"PILLOW BARRIER TO THE QUEEN. SALLY, OF THE HOUSE OF HALL. CROWN BARRIER TO THE QUEEN. SANDRA, OF THE HOUSE OF DAVIS."

There they are, little first graders, coming out of each door at the far end of the gym. Sandra has the crown. It glitters on a white pillow that she holds perfectly still in front of her—because Mrs. Moore will kill her if she lets it move.

Silence.

Now a new fanfare.

LADIES AND GENTLEMEN. HER MAJESTY, THE QUEEN OF MAY. CINDY LOUISE, OF THE HOUSE OF BURTON.

And oh, Katie Dee! I can't tell you what Cindy looked like! I don't know whether to start with that dress, so white, and so huge, and so beautiful... or her gloves that came all the way to her elbows, or with her smile, that looked like the whole sun the way it is high up in summer was shining from inside her face and it just kept shining out through her eyes, not moving from her king, while she kept walking along that floor toward him. I could never smile at anybody the way she smiled at him.

She got to the throne. She knelt. He took a step down from the platform toward her. Little Sandra Davis tottered up a step toward him. He lifted the silver crown and held it above her. Someone held a microphone in front of his mouth. He said:

"Cindy, of the House of Burton. I hereby crown you, Queen of May."

Very carefully, he set the crown on her head. Then he went down beside her, she rose, and, arm and arm, Jim Day and Cindy Burton stepped up, stepped up again, and finally sat on their thrones.

The Mayfate could begin.

And it did. Except I thought it was crummy.

I mean, all that time the sixth and seventh grades had spent building the Alamo out of paper mache, you would have expected something really special. And every grade sent people for soldiers—we sent Billy Wayne Williams, Jim Tomlinson, and Tommy Ford—so we were expecting a great battle. They had practiced for six weeks! I kept wondering who the Mexicans were going to be, and if they would have Ramon Garcia be Santa Anna; but he told me once he was just supposed to be a dancer in the square dance scene. And we didn't even know what to make of it when the soldiers came back and told us they didn't get to fight at all. But still, we thought there would at least be Davy Crockett, waving Ole Betsy up on the wall as the Mexicans came to bayonet him.

Nothing like that.

Nothing at all really.

Here's all there was about the Alamo:

The whole gym went completely dark. It was almost scary. You couldn't hear anything except some of the kids giggling and beginning to scuffle and fight, and Mrs. Moore's voice off somewhere shushing them. While it was dark you could hear heavy things being shoved around, on the end of the gym floor opposite where the Royal Party was sitting.

Then finally some lights came on under the basket down there. It was at the far wall, a dark blue light, with a couple of light bulbs stuck in the wall, so, against the blue, it looked like two stars, maybe in the early morning. Up against that was the outline of the Alamo. And I will say this: with all the net wire and crud gunk that Gretchen said it took—see, they made it at her house, because her sister is in the seventh grade—it did turn out big. The top of the little tower on the front of it hid the basketball goal from where we were. Then, as it got a little lighter, you could see bales of hay that were the walls. Maybe five or six bales high, all extending toward center court.

Like, we were on the inside, looking out.

The soldiers didn't do anything!

They just lay on the bales of hay, or on the floor, or sat with their backs to the front of the Alamo. And that's a shame—that they didn't do any fighting I mean—because they were made up real neat. They had bandages on, and crutches, and blue uniforms all torn, and their faces were bandaged too. But they just sat perfectly still, like they had been fighting a long time, and were hurt.

Nobody said anything. Mrs. Moore had got the first graders quiet. Probably she had drowned them in the boys' locker room, under the stands.

I thought they would at least have somebody play Davy Crockett. Or Travis. But no. All they had was a senior boy, talking into a microphone off somewhere we couldn't see it, read so that the voice came over the loudspeaker. It was the letter Travis wrote, I guess, but they didn't even introduce it. He just read:

To the People of Texas & all Americans in the World—
Fellow Citizens and Compatriots—

I am besieged by a thousand or more of the Mexicans under Santa Anna. I have sustained a continual bombardment and cannonade for twenty four hours and have not lost a man. The enemy has demanded a surrender at discretion, otherwise the garrison are to be put to the sword, if the fort is taken. I have answered the demand with a cannon shot, & our flag still waves proudly from the walls. *I shall never surrender or retreat...*

Then there was a spotlight, right in the center of the gym, over the circle panther. On one side of the circle they had put about a ten foot high pole with the American flag, and on the other the Texas flag. In the middle was a big white sign, with black letters on it. The letters said:

In Honor of the Brave Men and Women Who Have Died in Defense of Liberty

That kind of got to me, because of Daddy, and I felt my eyes doing the thing they do whenever I think of him. But if you take deep breaths that goes away. It did this time, too, or would have, except that Mel Hooper still had to play. He has a silver cornet, that shines like he polishes it for hours every night. He stood at attention, and, very slow, played Taps. I guess that's what you call it. That ever so slow song when soldiers get buried.

When he finished, the light went out again.

And that was it for the Alamo.

All that practice. Talk about a waste.

It got a little better then, but in a strange way. When the spotlight came on, Maggie Darling was in the middle of it. She was, like I was saying before, a singer who came all the way from Ft. Worth, and who had made records (they said), but who had grown up in Midlothian, living (they said too) in by where the Millers live now.

She had gotten famous.

But she didn't look famous.

See, I expected somebody kind of glittery, with long hair, like the women you see on the game shows. But she was just this—I don't know, she just looked like a schoolteacher. She had on a print dress like Mrs. Nelson always wears, and her hair was plain mouse hair all short and boy cut. And she just sat in a straight chair with a guitar in her lap, looking like she was about to nibble on the microphone. Didn't even look up. Then, real slow, too slow I thought, she did that kind of pick-strum where she would pluck one bass string with her thumb and then pluck the three top strings with the tips of her first three fingers.

She did that much too long. It wasn't even fast enough to be a march. But then she kind of growled into the microphone— she had a real low voice for a girl, like maybe she had smoked too much, except she didn't look like anybody who had ever smoked—she growled:

There's a Yellow Rose in Texas
That I am going to see,
Nobody else could miss her
Not half as much as me...

71

Katie Dee I can't tell you how bad this was. I mean, to be embarrassed. I kept thinking, did they pay this woman money to come and just play real slow and look at the microphone or was it just that she was born in Midlothian and nobody wanted to tell her flat out how awful she sang/talked?

She cried so when I left her
It like to broke my heart
And if I ever find her
We never more will part.

And then, a very strange thing happened. I still can't explain it. But right at that moment Maggie Darling looked up, and looked at both sides of the gym at all those top half of body shadows packed in there, which I know she couldn't see or tell who anybody was—she just looked up and smiled.

It was the best smile I ever saw.

It was a better smile even than Cindy Burton gave to Jim Day. Because that was an excitement smile, and this one was... I don't know. But she smiled it. This side got the smile. That side got the smile. The royal party got the smile. And when she looked at this side she said:

She's . . .

And when she looked at that side she said:

the...

And then, she nodded forward and sang:

Sweetest little rosebud, that Texas ever knew
Her eyes are bright as diamonds
They sparkle like the dew...

When she sang that, Katie Dee, everybody in the gym started singing along with her. And it wasn't even in the program! I mean, not as though everybody was singing loud, just loud enough to be heard over her soft guitar, but still singing.

While she just kept playing that steady beat, with her thumb and first three fingers.

You can talk about your Clementine and sing of Rosalie...
But the Yellow Rose of Texas is the only girl for me.

Then she did it again.

She's the sweetest little rosebud
That Texas ever knew...

Only with the chording hand, this time, she made a little gesture. And everyone stood up. I swear it was like we were in church.

Of course Mama says that in Texas, Texas history *is* church... But still!

So there we were, all singing, royal party too, while this mousy little woman just kept smiling her smile and every now and then having to make us all be quiet so she could sing a verse. Which she knew all of them of course, but I still thought, how stupid, that she can do something that is obviously this easy, and still get paid money!

Suddenly the lights came up. They had pulled the Alamo back out of the way and two rows of fourth and fifth grade kids, the boys with blue jeans and plaid shirts, girls with those old timey looking dresses, started marching out toward center court, weaving around and through the bales of hay.

"Y'all clap now!" said Maggie Darling, and of course the

crowd did. And when that happened the kids started to square dance. They locked arms and whirled around, and would have done pretty good because after all they had practiced this for seven weeks and why wouldn't you know it after that long.

So, I thought, maybe it's not going to be too bad after all.

Except for what Maggie Darling did then. I swear, Katie Dee, she did it.

Like, I'm going to make this up?

She put down her guitar—which wasn't necessary because by now the whole crowd was singing so loud you couldn't hear it anyway, all those people clapping and stomping and whatever, the same verse, over and over—but she put that guitar down, walked straight toward the throne, and held both arms straight out toward Jim Day!

I thought I would die.

I thought he would die.

You could see him blushing.

But I'll say this for him: he didn't blush long. He got right up off that throne, and in two or three bounces he was down there with her. The teachers on the sidelines, all what seemed like ten thousand or so of them, were looking at each other like the gym had caught on fire.

He bowed and she curtseyd, he kind of bent and hitched up one leg and they went square dancing down the court. After a while they got to the fourth graders, who were now being accompanied by a bunch of third graders playing the flutophones, except you couldn't hear them because all the people in the gym were falling over laughing and whistling and stomping and clapping and singing, for probably the fifty thousandth time by now:

She's the sweetest little rosebud

That Texas ever knew...

But that still wasn't enough for crazy Maggie Darling, who, when Jim Day kind of whirled her off from him, didn't come back, and grabbed of all people Gretchen's father! The poor guy was kneeling down with his movie camera trying to get a shot of Gretchen dancing, so when this wild spinning mousewoman grabbed his elbow and started tugging him up, he almost dropped the camera. And you can imagine what the crowd did then. Hoots. Everybody yelling.

"Dance with her Charlie! Dance with her, Charlie!"

He did. Not too good, but he tried.

Well, after a while it was just out of control. Everybody was out on the court. Months of practice, all ruined. Everybody laughing and going crazy like wild indians. I caught sight of Mrs. Moore once. She was just walking up and down on the sideline, shaking her head, shrugging her shoulders like and looking the way old people get when they lose their minds.

"Y'all's turn now!"

There she was, standing in front of us! I don't mean Mrs. Moore. I mean Maggie Darling! She was right in front of Jeremy and me and believe me I was terrified.

"Now I know y'all have on those big dresses and everything but y'all can still dance."

"No we can't!" somebody yelled out.

I think it was a tenth grader.

"C'mon now, c'mon now, y'all follow me!"

Then she hauled Jeremy up!

Poor Jeremy looked worse than he had with the corsage. But he followed her, and I somehow followed him, and then I saw what we were doing. It wasn't too bad. We just formed a big row, single file, with everybody's hand on the waist of the person in front of us. And that way, a giant formal royal party Maysnake, we just wobbled our way around the floor. It was the loudest, craziest thing I had ever seen. Down toward the Alamo, around the haybales, up under the scorer's table, Jeremy turning around laughing this stupid laugh every half minute or so, and me with the tips of my fingers snagged just inside his cummerbund. The shoes—oh the things I called those shoes, which probably were like two screwdrivers ripping up the gym floor but if everybody else could do it why not me? And people said they had to revarnish the gym floor every year after Mayfate anyway.

I guess the thing I remember most about that whole dance, is—well, two things. Passing Reverend Bryant three times, each time him going in a different direction, each time his face more red and more like he was going to have a heart attack, and each time him with another woman. All of them laughing just as much as he was, linked up elbow and elbow, whirling around and trying not to fall down.

And the other thing, after it went on like it would go on all night, somehow, everybody, knowing to look up at the scorer's platform, and there in a spotlight Maggie Darling. The lights went down, everybody out of breath and yellingsinging at once; then a spotlight came on. It was perfectly round behind her, as though she was outlined against a giant full white spotlight moon. She had a microphone and into it she said, real slow:

And the Yellow Rose of Texas
Will be mine
For evvvvvv errrr
More!

There was just this moment when, believe it or not, everyone was completely silent. You could hear a pin drop. And in that moment Maggie Darling leaned forward and said into the microphone:

"I tell you. Y'all are good!"

Then she threw back her head and laughed, and the lights came on, and there was more clapping and yelling and applauding than you've ever heard before in your life.

Jeremy and I just stood and laughed too, and shook our heads at each other.

And that was my first Mayfate.

There were a few more acts, but they were nothing after that. It was all over about eleven thirty. The march out went fast, and was nothing to worry about after the entry march. During the march out you could have fallen on your face and nobody would have cared. Jeremy disappeared of course after we got to the foyer. But I did see Mama. She was out of breath too, and her eyes were all red. I wanted to go up to her, but there was a mob in the foyer. By the time I got to her she was hugging Mrs. Bergvall, who hugged her back. Mama was saying:

"That Alamo scene, Sue. I mean, that sign, and that scene..."

"We thought of you, Nancy. And we thought of Tom."

"He would have liked it, Sue. He loved that letter."

"I know."

"And it's a heckuva letter, isn't it?"

Mrs. Nelson had her eyes all watery then, and mine got that way too, because I knew they were talking about Daddy.

"Yes. Yes, it's a heckuva letter."

They hugged again, and I felt maybe I should just go outside.

Which, it took me a while to get there, there were so many people.

But it was worth it. It was a warm May night, and all the

stars in the world were out, and, walking back behind the gym, it smelled like you were in a flower shop. The people smoking stood on the street, so I just walked slow to the Stephenson's fence, where their mean dog came barking and yapping over to me, and ploughed to a stop, and smelled me through the net wire, and then decided I could stay. I guess I seemed strange to him, there, almost midnight, a girl in a formal dress.

Sometimes you just want to be out away from people, you know?

So I stood there a long time, not really thinking about Daddy, because I was only six and that was some years ago when he— or rather when the plane he was piloting—you know.

But I felt like I might get into one of those moods again, when I heard footsteps and kind of whirled around. It was Jeremy! He didn't have on his tuxedo jacket. His tie was kind of loosened.

"What are you doing here?"

"I don't know. It's kind of crowded back there."

"Your mother's looking for you."

"Oh. I better come then."

"Yeah, I just..." He shrugged. "I just thought I ought to tell you, thanks for asking me to be your Duke."

"That's all right."

"It was great."

And I started to speak, but I couldn't. Because... do you know what happened then, Katie Dee? He kissed me! Jeremy. He kissed me! Right there where the corner post of the Stephenson's yard is next to that weed grown lot by the First Presbyterian Church. He just... stepped forward, and kind of cupped my chin with the palm of his hand, and, breath warm and that shock of hair fallen down against my nose—he kissed me. Then he stepped back. We just kind of looked at each other for a second.

I don't think either one of us knew anything to say.

Then: "I'll tell your mother you're coming."

"All... all right." And he went back to the gym.

When I finally found Mama she had started toward the truck. She had a bowl of potato salad in her arms. I don't know where she got it. It just seems though, that, whenever Mama goes to anywhere with a lot of other women, a meeting or whatever, she leaves with a big bowl of potato salad.

"Where were you, Katie?"

"I was... nowhere, just... nowhere."

She walked toward me and took my shoulder with her not-bowl-of-potato-salad hand: "Are you all right?"

"Yeah, I'm all right."

"Katie?!"

"What?"

She kept looking at me as though I was different or something. Then she just shook her head. "You look like something happened to you. Did it?"

"No."

"Huh. All right, then. What did you think of the May Fete?"

"I thought it was a great Mayfate."

"Fete."

"It sounds like 'fate' to me, Mama"

Then she kind of looked at me again, and tousled my hair, and smiled, so that you could see she had been crying there with Mrs. Nelson.

"Well. Maybe 'fate' is right, girl. Maybe 'fate' is better."

And we went home.

Yours faithfully,

Katie Haw

The Biggest Catfish
in the World

The Biggest Catfish
in the World

May 14, 1967
Midlothian, Texas

Dear Katie Dee,

A week after the Mayfate—which made me kind of famous, I guess—Mama and I went fishing. I know it was just a week later because it was Friday, May 12 and that was a date everybody in Midlothian was going to remember for a long time. And not just because it was a week after I got to be in the Mayfate.

We had finished walking through the wheat, which looked great because of all the rain and still hadn't gotten ripe, but had long, full heads. Nobody had planted corn yet, and that was bad, but the rain just didn't let up this spring. Good for wheat, bad for corn planting. Anyway we were feeling good about the wheat, and Mama said we should take a day on the creek fishing to reward ourselves. Not our little creek that runs through the pasture, but Long Branch, which has huge, deep, straight-up-and-down dirt walls and some fishing holes almost ten feet deep with water backed up from Spring Hills Lake.

We got up early, just before sunup, had bacon and eggs for breakfast, and then packed some hot dogs to cook down on the creek. I herded the beagles into the cab of the pickup while Mama got the fishing stuff ready. It's four miles on the farm to market road to Burton's gate, and after you go through that you have to bounce and slide over pasture—we almost got stuck twice—to the point where there's too much undergrowth to drive.

83

The dogs yelped and scratched and licked and jumped around, Mama yelling at them every other word or so and me remembering what they would be like at the end of the day, two dog rags that could stretch out in the back of the truck and never move all the way back. If they came back. Sometimes Annie and Spud slid off on a creek chase and didn't show themselves again for two days.

We made our way down into the creek bed, which is pretty shallow up by Burton's, and started walking along it. Both of us had on high, water tight boots so we could wade through the shallow pools. Every half mile or so came white limestone outcroppings. I like to sit on those, and hunt for iron ore nuggets. It was a good time of the morning, the sun just up over Burton's barn off to the east, roosters crowing, and hawks circling over the new baled grain fields bordering Long Branch.

Spud opened up first. I don't know how he could have gotten so far down the creek. He bayed more like a hippopotamus than a beagle—bayoooo bayooo bayooo, and Annie joined in then, with her mouth Mama says is too broken to be a good hound dog mouth, I have no idea what that means.

"Listen to that! Sounds like a yard dog."

"A dog is a dog, Mama."

"Huh."

"Listen. They're really frantic now."

"Yeah. They think they're hot stuff."

"You think they'll catch him this quick?"

"Are you kidding? That's a swamp rabbit. He's probably halfway back to us by now."

"He's coming this way?"

"Be quiet. Keep watching."

We did, and sure enough in about five minutes the rabbit came jerking and bouncing along on the other side of the bank, crisscrossing the stream, darting into this and that gnarl of roots that current had exposed, hiding in the thistle pile, his little bright eye round as a dime, shining smart and I-know-I'm-hidden out from a tangle of brush.

Annie and Spud were tearing up the air half a mile away, and going in the wrong direction.

"Stupid dogs," Mama whispered.

We waited until the rabbit had made his way along, and then we headed off to where the holes were twenty or thirty feet wide, and the current hardly moved.

There is a good place there, another bigger limestone spread. The water is dark green, deep looking, with a few fallen and rotten pecan trees sticking up in the mud and shallows of the pond edges. Squirrels rattled and yelled at us, and chased each other up and down the trunks of trees that grew so high over the pond that their branches intertwined. As the sun climbed the light began to streak yellow-green and weird patterned through the trees and creek brambles—and after the squirrels quieted down you could hear nothing at all except the burbling of the water downstream, a few crows cawing, and some small bullfrogs in the reeds across from us.

Down in the deep part of a creek, when it's real still, you feel like you need to whisper. I don't know why, but you just do.

Mama bent over and watched as I tied the hook on.

"Up, through—now around, and loop it six times. That's it. One more, Katie. Yeah. Now pull it tight. Good. Good ole' hangman's noose of a hook knot. Not any fish getting away, not today."

"Give me a worm."

"Here."

"No, that's a slug."

"So?"

"I hate those things."

"I'm not asking you to marry it, silly. Just put it on your hook. What is this, a worm popularity contest?"

"It looks so gross."

"Who cares? Throw it down there."

I got the yucchy fat white thing with its horny yellow head and tiny hairs sticking out and speared it so that juice poppled out onto the hook and dribbled around my fingers.

"This is so gross."

"You said that."

"Well, it is."

"Get your hook in the water. I want to build a fire."

"Middle of May and you're building a fire."

"For the coffee, silly."

"I know that. I still think it's stupid, the things grownups drink. Wine. Beer. Coffee. Nothing that tastes good."

She opened up the army green and battered knapsack and got out a metal coffee pot that had been put in the fire so often its bottom was blackened. She also got out an orange Nehi soda.

"Here. So your teeth can rot."

"Good," I answered, popping it open. "You didn't bring any Fire Stix, did you?"

"Please, I have my standards."

"Mama..."

"Will you put the bait in the water? I want to fish this week sometime."

"Yeah, so we can bury ourselves in the wheat field again tomorrow."

I adjusted the white and red bobber so that the bait would hang about eight feet down in the water, just above the bottom. Then I mashed the casting button, held it hard, and drew back.

"Not in the middle, Katie. Try to get it over by the far pecan tree, where those limbs are sticking up out of the water. Just not too far, because you'll get hung up."

"OK."

Straight over the top, and let the button go... now.

Plop.

"Good. Good cast."

And there was the bobber, popping its red plastic stem straight up as soon as the sinker had gotten to the right depth.

"Now, to live a little."

She got some straw and twigs, and a few larger branches. After a while a little fire crackled in a small heap of undergrowth there beside us on the rock porch of the creek bottom.

The coffee did smell kind of good when it got going, but not as good as my Nehi, which was now half gone.

I wished for Fire Stix.

"When will we harvest the wheat?"

"About three weeks. We ought to get forty bushels to the acre."

She put her knapsack behind her, wedged it against the rock creek bank, and leaned back. The tin cup of coffee between her stretched out legs steamed; she got a kind of dreamy look. I did too, I guess. We just kind of sat there, enjoying the day.

The bobber disappeared.

"Wait a minute!"

My hand had jerked to the rod, which was lying by my feet; I almost kicked it down into the water.

The red top popped by up out of the water again.

"I should have had him!"

She just shook her head.

"Wait," she whispered.

It sat still on the water for a second, then jerked off to the right, in the direction of the roots sticking out of the bank; then it disappeared under, nothing but wave circles spreading out where the red spot had been.

Then it came back up again.

"Bream," she said. "Or something else little."

"How do you know that?"

"If it's a big carp or a catfish you'll know it. Look. There he goes again, just playing with it."

Sure enough, the bobber darted around, one direction for a foot or so, then back another way.

We watched it for a while, never getting a bite good enough to hang on to. Finally I pulled it in; no bait.

"Here, use a red worm this time, and cast over to the right."

Spud started bellowing far up the creek to our right while I was re-baiting the hook.

"How did they get past us?"

"I don't know. They must have been up in the field. They're almost back where we left the truck. Poor things. Look."

And here came the rabbit, working his way past us from right to left, along with the flow of the creek, hiding in this patch and that, with still a mile or so between him and the beagles, who, again, were going in the wrong direction.

"They won't give up, though," she whispered, after the swamp rabbit had disappeared on down the creek. "Texas dogs—too dumb to quit."

I cast over to the right this time, just at the base of a huge pecan tree whose roots were half exposed; the trunk must have been three feet thick, and it went up and up and overtopped even the other trees. The bobber hit the water, righted itself stem up, and almost immediately disappeared.

"How'd the little sucker get over there so quick?" Mama asked, stubbing her cigarette out on the rock beside her.

"I don't know."

This time the cork didn't come up.

The tiny dot where the fishing line entered the water started moving, slow, still moving, down the creek.

The reel turned slowly, line playing itself out, a quiet grinding noise with the little handle turning just above my thumb.

She sat forward.

It was going faster now.

Still no bobber; just a dot, now heading fast toward the end of the pool, the reel whirring fast.

"Get him! Get him Katie!"

I jerked as hard as I could; the rod tip jumped up a foot or so and then wham, it felt like truck had it; I grabbed the reel handle but couldn't stop it; I got the rod in both hands then, braced myself, and heaved backward. It turned the fish a little, but only a little. The line kept peeling out toward a bunch of ferns down where the creek narrowed and got faster.

"I can't get him! He's too strong!"

"Come on! Don't pull too hard!"

"He's getting away!"

"No, he isn't!"

"He's going for those ferns!"

"Let him. Come on."

She was on her feet then, slipping a little, helping me up while I still had tight hold of the rod and the fish kept taking more line with him.

"You pull too hard you'll break the line!"

"What is that thing?"

"I don't know, but it isn't a bream."

We were both holding onto the rod now, trying to follow the fish and hold the rod tip up, splashing a little into the mud slick side of the creek. About ten yards down the rock gave way to mud, and there we had given ourselves a little slack.

"Get it good in your hands!"

I had my right hand firm on the reel and my left braced above the cork handle. A good jerk got the fish turned toward us; you could see the line moving back toward the center of the pool.

"Get him! Get him! Nice and strong, just steady."

I could get one turn on the handle; then another; then another... the dot where line entered water came toward us, jerked away, came toward us...

"That's right, Katie. Move him in. Move him in..."

We were both ankle deep in water now, tall reeds surrounding us. A bullfrog the size of a rabbit splashed into the water with a grunt and a croak; sweat dripped into my eyes. "Come on; keep turning that thing..."

"I'm getting him."

"I know honey; keep it up, keep..." And then we saw the fish.

"Oh my God," she whispered. I didn't say anything.

It was the biggest fish I had ever seen; it was longer than Mama. I don't know how long it was; but there was just this blackgray body, all glistening in the sun at the top of the water and a monster mouth that could have eaten a cow—I swear, it looked like a cow, this fish... and it just hung there in the water, silent, not moving, for an instant... then it arched itself, whacked the water with a slap of its giant flat body so that spray splashed down soaking us... and was gone. The rod jerked, the line shot straight up, the red bobber tangled itself in a tree above us... and the fish had disappeared.

The water in front of us began to cloud with creek bottom dirt.

She and I just stood for a second; she had her arm around me. We looked at each other. Our mouths were open.

"Did you see that?"

"I don't know," I answered. "What *was* that thing?"

"I don't... I don't know."

Then she laughed. We both laughed. We stood, drenched with water, sweating, gnats and mosquitoes wailing around us... just shaking our heads and laughing.

"I knew," she said, hands on my shoulders, trying to get her breath, "I knew that there were catfish in this creek five feet long."

"That fish was five feet long?"

"That fish was as long as you are, my baby, and you are five feet long."

"Oh my Lord."

"Oh my Lord, is right."

"That thing could have... Mama that thing could have eaten us!"

"That fish could have eaten Fort Worth. That fish could have... hey, come on, let's get out of the water. He might come back."

We made our way back, dripping and laughing. The pool was perfectly still now, except for the mud spreading out. My shirt had been soaked, and so had her blouse beneath her jacket. We were just in that kind of excited way you get when both of you want to talk at once. I would start to say something, and then she would be nodding her head and saying yes yes yes but when you slipped I tried to catch you then I knew it was big but I and then yes I knew it was big too but I thought if we and I never had any idea that the thing could I mean not in *this* creek not really—now if it were the big lake, then maybe...

And that's when we heard it.

I still remember hearing it.

Low in the distance. A soft, rumbling sound. Gentle, just to get your attention. Then once again. Crows kept cawing, circling. Bob Burton must have turned his cows into the pasture. Back up toward the barn you could hear them, and his old bull that was harmless, coming out with a bellow every now and then. That and a few crickets chirping around the edges of the pond.

There was no wind. It was perfectly still.

And then that rumbling sound again.

"What's that?"

"I don't know," she answered. "I don't know. Listen."

Silence for a while. Then the sound. Hard to tell where from. Just rumbling. In the air.

"What is it?"

She shook her head, lips straight together, a line of mouth, a thin line like when she thinks real hard.

"Listen."

A little louder.

"Wait."

"Where are you going?"

"Wait here. I'll be back."

She slid off to the right, walking straight up, a not-worried but-not-OK-either walk that grownups have. She had to go up the creek about fifty yards to cross. It was still waist deep there, and she held her hands above her head as the water got up around her hips. She slipped a couple of times; the rock bottom there must have been moss covered. Then she had to climb hard, pulling on roots and dead branches to get to the top of the steep bank. After she disappeared into the undergrowth at the top of the bank I sat down.

It was half a minute before she came back into sight.

The noise kept coming.

Again, soft and low; but not stopping, either. There was never a time when you couldn't hear it.

When she got back, she shook her head. "I don't understand it," she said.

"What is it?"

"I don't know."

"It sounds like thunder."

"Yes, it does. But the sky is clear in the northwest."

"What could it be, then? It's got to be thunder."

She looked at her watch. "It's nine thirty in the morning. Nine thirty in the morning, and the sky is perfectly clear. But that sounds like it's coming from…"

The noise kept coming.

"Let's go," she said.

"What is it?"

"Come on. Get the stuff. Let's go."

"Mama?"

"Come on."

We walked very fast then. She had the knapsack with the coffee pot in it, and I took the rod and some of the lunch stuff.

"What about Spud and Annie?"

"They'll be OK."

"Are you sure?"

"I'm sure. Here; watch the branch."

"What are we doing?"

"We're climbing the bank; we have to get into Burton's pasture."

"We're not going back along the creek?"

"No. Too slow."

And sure enough, she headed up the bank above us, right through rough thistles and undergrowth. We had to tear our way through thorns, and every now and then she let a branch swing back and whap me in the face. We were both on the lookout for snakes; spider webs hung huge and patterned and covered us like tiny threads of tissue paper as we climbed, scrambled, dirt-slogged our way under brambles and up that steep bank. I had never tried to climb out of the creek this way before, especially not carrying all the stuff.

"Wait, Mama."

"Katie we need to go."

"What is it? Why are we hurrying so?"

"The weather."

"Is it going to rain?"

She was almost to the top of the bank, holding on to a root, her boot wedged inside some bank hole an armadillo or raccoon had dug.

"Yeah. I think so."

"So what's the big deal? We'll just get wet."

"Come on."

And with that she pulled herself out over the bank; I grabbed the same root she had been holding and hauled myself up, while I could hear her tromping through the weeds and Johnson grass that separated the creek from Burton's pasture.

She had torn away a path through the undergrowth, so that I could get through it a little easier, although I still felt prickled and torn all over from those tiny thorn branch threads that never let you go, that stick in your clothes and unravel with you as you push along through them.

Finally I broke out of the brush into the pasture.

Then I saw it.

Coming up out of the southeast, where storms never come from.

Right up over Burton's red barn.

"Oh Mama..."

"Yeah."

We were both breathing hard and sweating. We couldn't stop

looking at the cloud.

It's very hard to describe it, except that you could see it getting closer, fast. The sky above us, and back behind us, was that normal perfect blue a good May day with the sun higher and hotter all the time, making the overhead white blue with heat. But all in front of us now, beginning to come around us on either side, this purple-black band with snake cloud streaks circling, rising, falling, tearing apart, smoke-flowing back together—this thing hung there halfway up the sky like a wave. Lightning bolts sizzled down every second or so, there, over by Holmes' barn, and back there, whack, a crack of lightning just beyond the hackberry hedge row of our back field—and all the time boom boom boooom, the thunder coming and never stopping, like fifty big army airplanes were coming toward us.

As though God had dropped an anvil across the storm, because the purple top was string straight, not one tuft of cloud sticking over that line that separated the black storm from the blue sky.

And that line kept coming toward us. Getting its storm arms around us.

Brooom. Broooom.

Crack. Lightning. Crack crack.

"Let's go, Baby."

She didn't have to tell me twice.

We were a half mile from the truck.

Mama used to play basketball, and other sports. She never talks about it, but she did. She has long legs, too. We walked fast for about a hundred yards, but soon we both knew we would have to run. You didn't have to say it. We both started kind of jogging at the same time. I knew it was a long way. It was hard with the bag of food in one hand and the rod in the other; you couldn't swing your arms right.

After we had run a little way she stopped. We both stared at the cloud.

How can I describe it? I guess—well, if the horizon, straight in front of you, is nine o'clock, and right above the top of your head is twelve o'clock—then the top of this thing was at eleven o'clock.

And in a few minutes it would be covering the sun.

"Leave the pole and food here," she whispered.

She put her knapsack on the ground.

"What'll happen to them?"

"Nothing. Let's go."

We could run better then. It was like doing laps at school. Close your fists tight; keep your breathing regular. The little sharp pain tears at your side, ribs ripping away from your stomach…breathe deep, breathe deep.

There was a turn in the creek. We went around it, keeping pace together, not breathing too hard—there, there's the truck, a couple of hundred yards away.

And very quickly the world went dark. Like twilight.

Within about half a minute all the yard lights come on: Burton's, Holmes', ours way off in the distance. The roosters started crowing.

I couldn't believe what I saw—that strange still pasture; not a breath of wind blowing; and night that wasn't night just hanging over the whole world.

Then Burtons' barn disappeared. It just wasn't there anymore. Where it had been, and stretching as far as you could see in either direction, a gray curtain, like a dust cloud. It was about a hundred yards beyond the truck.

"How you doing, Katie?"

"Fine," I said, not panting too hard. "I wish I didn't have these... heavy boots on."

"I know. Listen baby, you have a good sprint left in you?"

"I think so."

"OK, let's race. Go!"

I took off as fast as I could then, bending low, tearing out like I did for third base four days before; except this time she was just behind me.

"Go baby go baby go baby... gonna catchya gonna catchya gonna catchya..."

My side was hurting really bad then, and sweat stung my eyes so bad I had to keep wiping them every other stride.

"I need to stop a minute..."

"No you don't... not too far now..."

We had to jump the prickly pears and chugholes, some of them with water still standing.

"It hurts, it hurts..."

"Come on, we're almost there!"

Finally we made it. I crashed into the truck and bent over the fender for a few seconds, panting like a dog, trying to keep from throwing up. Her arm snaked around my waist. Neither of us could talk.

"Come on."

I got in first, sliding under the steering wheel and on over to the door, my forehead pressed against the window. She just had time to turn on the key before the rain hit. It wasn't like a few drops, and then a few more drops, and like that—it was wham, like the world's hugest water balloon had broken right above us, a million billion gallons drenching down on one little truck.

"Let's go!" I screamed, as loud as I could, still barely able to hear myself.

She just shook her head.

"Can't see!"

And you couldn't. Not a foot. Just water. Pounding, shaking

the truck, running in through cracks in the windows...we scrunched together in the middle of the seat; I bent over and put my head in her lap.

Then the noise changed.

Imagine, you're in a car, and somebody starts pouring gravel on the top of it. Then rocks. Then bigger rocks, from fifty feet up, thousands of them. Bang bang bang bang...

"Mama!"

"Sssh. Keep your head down."

"What is it? What is it?"

"Keep your head down, just keep your head in my lap... keep your head down..."

But I couldn't. I jerked up and saw the windshield cracking. A huge, fine, spider web draped over it, and more little weblines kept spreading, centering out from every rock explosion, pow, pow, louder than locomotive engines roaring right on top of us.

"Mama!"

She pulled me down hard and kept my head buried in her lap. I could feel her palm cupped over the back of my neck. My nose was buried in the upholstery, and all I can remember was that terrible noise, and the truck shaking and bouncing, and it never stopping, knowing that once the windshield shattered the rocks would hit us and kill us. I kept thinking it was starting; I kept feeling them on my back, and I wanted so bad to run, but there was no place to go; you just had to keep breathing, and crying, and breathing, and waiting while God shook us and pounded us.

I don't know how long it lasted.

Finally I could hear her telling me that it was all right now, and I realized that she wasn't shouting. When I raised up again I saw there was rain falling, but a kind of soft rain. We weren't shaking anymore; everything had gotten bright and dripping.

The sun came out. It kept raining for a few more minutes, even in bright sunshine; then even that rain stopped.

Outside of the truck the ground was covered with the strangest things you've ever seen. They were everywhere, lying littered in pools of rainwater. Ice chunks, but not jagged—smooth polished balls, cold in your hand, frozen swirled circles spiraling inside them.

Mama and I just walked around the truck for a time, not talking, just picking these things up and looking at them.

"Come on."

I got back in. She started the engine. It was bouncy going over the pasture, and once we almost got stuck. She had to rock the truck, gunning it forward, slamming it in reverse, and letting it go backward and straight again twice.

I don't remember much about the ride back home except that the fencerow trees looked so strange, shredded, all their leaves gone, the branches black, twisted, glistening and broken.

We stopped at Cindy Burton's house. It's a big two-story house. All of the windows had been broken out, and the shingles were shattered, black tarpaper spots dotting the big white walls now.

Mrs. Burton was out in the yard. We stopped and got out, and the three of us kind of made a human knot in the center of the yard. We were all crying, me having started up again, not really knowing why, just not able to stop.

Finally I walked into their house. Cindy wasn't there, and the house was empty. It felt like a deserted house. Strange some of the things you will do or remember; but I walked upstairs, as though drawn there, and her Mayfate queen gown was lying on the bed. I don't know what it was doing there. Her dresser was covered in pictures, and there was a gold clock in a glass case. But beyond Cindy's dresser the windows had been shattered, and the floor was littered with glass and water.

Sometimes you want to get things out of your mind, I guess. Even now when people ask me about the hailstorm—because when they say *the* hailstorm they mean that one and there will never be another like it—even now, what comes to my mind, for no particular reason, is that deserted window broken room, and Cindy's beautiful dress lying on that bed like a huge white bear.

Going home was the hardest thing, of course.

Mama parked the truck on the east side of the farm. We walked out into the field.

The wheat was shredded salad. Nothing in the field came up higher than our ankles.

We stood there for a long time, the sun hot now, straight up over our heads.

Then she knelt down, put her face in her hands, and cried.

It had been such a beautiful field of wheat.

I stood with my hands on her shoulders, not knowing how I could stop her from crying. I guess we would still be there if some movement over on the far side of the field... the north side... hadn't caught my eye.

I looked up. There were the two beagles, white flag tails waving, working their way toward us through all that fodder and dying wet foliage.

Mama saw them at the same time I did, and we both had to laugh. You couldn't *not* laugh, not when you saw what Spud had in his mouth.

"Those stupid dogs," she said, just kind of sputtering now, kicking the wheat garbage and wiping her eyes. "Those stupid dogs caught that rabbit."

And they had. And there they went with it, as airy as you please, just trotting home from their day's work, passing within a few yards from us and never blinking an eye, that old bleeding rag of a rabbit clamped firm in Spud's big mouth.

"Texas dogs," I said.

She nodded. "Texas dogs."

She laughed again and shook her head.

And we went home.

Always,

Katie Haw

Ballgame

Ballgame

June 18, 1967
Midlothian, Texas

Dear Katie Dee,
    We played Cedar Hill three nights ago.
    What a game.
    It's like this, Katie Dee. I'm real mad when we get there, because I've forgotten my bat, and Mama won't take the truck back to get it.
    "It's the only one I can hit with."
    "I'm not driving ten miles back to the farm so you can get a bat."
    "But these are too heavy."
    "The other kids use them."
    "They're just not right. I want my bat."
    "I'm sorry, Katie, but that's too far. The game would be half over when I got back."
    And she's got that look about her, so I give up. I want my bat though because it's—well, it's that bat I wrote you about. The bat that I play ball with out by the chimney.
    But there's nothing to do. So I wait while we drive around looking for a place to park, and finally roll over a ditch and stop with the bumper up next to the wire fence that runs along the left field line.
    It's a summer night; you wouldn't believe it, but the whole town is there to watch. Cedar Hill is about ten miles north of

Midlothian, and it seems like everybody in both towns has come out to watch. The ballpark is right in the center of town. There are three rows of seats on the first base side, and five rows of seats behind us players on the third base side. It's all lit up like a carnival. They're selling snowcones behind home plate. A bunch of women are in there, working the cone machine and selling cokes and peanuts and candy bars. The women all are big and have big arms and sweaty faces, with their glasses steamed up. The booth is lit by yellow light: on the outside of it is written:

SUPPORT YOUR PTA

And I want a snowcone too, but Darryl, when I walk over to where the players are, says we can't get one.

"Why not?"

"They don't want you eatin' nothin' before the game."

"But a snowcone won't hurt anybody. Look, there's some kids outside the fence getting them. How come they get 'em and we don't? Like that's fair?"

"Gonna take us all to the Dairy Queen anyway after the game."

"Really?"

"Sure, get you anything you want."

"Oh."

"Get to ride in the truck, too."

The sun has been down for a while now. The lights are on and you can hear gnats up buzzing around them. People sit on the hoods of pickup trucks. I've lost sight of my Mama, and finally I see her; she's gotten back in the cab of the truck, watching from there. She doesn't like baseball very much, I think. Anyway, I'm not doing much of anything, just leaning on the fence and trying to get my socks straight, when Mr. Caldwell comes up to me. He must be a hundred years old.

You know that silver sheet-metal your mother uses to wrap

roasts in before she puts them in the oven? Imagine a ball of that, all crinkled up. Now make it dark brown, and somehow work the root of a cigar into it. That's what his face looks like. You can hardly see his eyes at all, they're so squinty.

He gestures that I'm supposed to come over to him. He puts his hand on my shoulder, pushes back his straw hat, and spits. Then he says to me:

"Don't try to kill it, honey. Just meet it."

"All right."

He nods, and goes away.

We have a meeting then, out behind third base. The coach goes over all of the signals: bunt, steal, squeeze play, all of that stuff. Bunt is the bill of the cap, steal is he takes off his cap and rubs his hair, squeeze play is he rubs his hand over his belt buckle. I get a look at Darryl. He's standing in the back of the group, staring at center field. Great. Like he's really going to know what to do if he ever gets one of those signals.

"Play ball!" the umpire yells.

The umpire is Euless Ruskin, Bobby's dad. Everybody calls him Useless Ruskin but he isn't really useless in baseball because, since he's Bobby's dad, and Bobby is our catcher, he cheats for our team. Anything that our pitcher can throw that Bobby can catch in the air, Useless calls a strike. Last year there was some argument about that, and someone got a broken collarbone. A parent I mean, not a player. But Useless wouldn't quit umpiring, and so now the father of their first baseman gets to umpire when we go to Cedar Hill.

We all get knotted together in a little group now, holding our arms out, trying to touch each other's hands in the middle of this clump of kids. My socks, like I was telling you, keep coming down; they've gotten all wadded up inside my shoes. I want to undo the laces, but coach is yelling at us to be quiet.

"Listen up! Prayer now! Y'all be quiet!"

The players get quiet, but the people along the fences are shouting. Dogs bark like crazy in the yards of houses back beyond the streets, and people honk the horns of pickup trucks. Little clouds of cigar smoke are everywhere.

"It's game time again, oh Lord," coach yells. "Make us mindful of thy many mercies, and help us to win the game. Amen."

"Let's go!" everybody yells, and we head out to the field.

I get to play right field, probably because I'm new and they don't think I'm very good. In the little league they put all the bad players in right field. In the big leagues Henry Aaron plays right field. I think to myself that I'm Henry Aaron. Far in front of me, in the infield, our players throw the ball around. It's very light in the infield and very dark out where I am. There is only one light pole. I can see Darryl over in center field; he seems a mile away.

He looks back but doesn't wave.

To my left and behind me is an old bandstand. It's made out of red bricks. Some bigger kids, teenagers I guess, have gotten up there, giggling and smoking cigarettes. Little red points of fire look like fireflies, and the teenagers just shadows moving around on the bandstand as our pitcher throws a ball about five feet outside, and Bobby Ruskin catches it, and Useless calls it a strike.

Everybody yells; all of the car horns go off.

Nothing happens then for a while. Nobody hits the ball toward me. If they did, I couldn't catch it because it's so dark. Behind me, out behind the right field fence, is a house I keep looking at. It has a big porch, and the porch is lighted. Several people, all of them pretty old, sit on the porch. Two go back and forth in the swing while the other just rocks. They laugh, and talk. Then I start thinking about you, Katie Dee. It would be fun for us to play in that house, or on that porch. It's night, like now, and summer, like now, and our parents sit out on the porch talking. We're playing hide and seek, jumping off the wooden railing around the porch, into the flower beds. We get yelled at, but it's all right. Afterward they give us watermelon. We stay up very late.

Mama drives us home then. We get to ride in the back of the truck, after she tells us about a million times that we can't stand up. Then, out at the farm, we sleep in the yard on the iron bed with the beat up mattress and camping blankets. There are more stars than you ever dreamed of. There are shooting stars, so many that you finally lose count. After midnight you can hear train whistles in the distance.

Wouldn't that be fun, Katie Dee?

Finally we get to go in. Darryl bats first. He swings at the first three pitches and doesn't come close to any of them. The last one is, like, twenty feet above the catcher, and it whams off a two by four at the top of the backstop so hard a section of net wire falls down. Darryl swings at it anyway. He's out, of course, as soon as they finally find the stupid ball and throw it to first.

Darryl comes back to our dugout and spits in the sand. He looks at all of us and yells:

"He ain't got nothin! Kick his butt!"

Then he screams out at Acie Barker:

"You ragarm! You ain't got nothin. We gone kick you into next week!" Then he comes over and sits down by me.

"Right, Darryl," I tell him.

He just kind of glares.

"Shoot."

Boys.

It's the second inning before I get to bat, and that is kind of creepy. With so many people watching, I mean. I'm the only girl on the team, I guess. I don't know where all the rest of the girls in this stupid town are.

Their catcher is as tall sitting down as I am standing up. His wrists look like boards, or planks that are sweating, and it's pretty clear why nobody wants to hit off Acie Barker. He's got to be six feet tall. He's as broad as the whole mound is.

"Comebaby comebaby comebaby fire it in here! Easyhitter easyhitter easyhitter! Comebabycomebabycomebaby!"

I wish the catcher would shut up.

Umpire Euless Ruskin won't let me bat. He takes off the mask, steps back, and points at my middle. I'm just standing there, kicking that white rubber home plate with the sand blowing over it. He won't let me bat.

Our coach comes out.

"What's the matter?"

"She can't bat like that."

"Why not?"

"Shirt tail."

"What?"

"She's got to put in her shirt tail."

"What difference does that make?"

"Rules. That's in the rule book."

Our coach sells insurance, I think. Anyway he looks like the insurance salesman we used to go to in Atlanta. Useless is a farmer and he looks like—I don't know what Useless looks like.

He's tall, and has on his overalls behind his chest protector. He's skinny, and red-brown, and almost as wrinkled as Mr. Caldwell. He doesn't have much hair on top of his head, but strange white bunches of it sticking out everywhere you don't expect it. It's like he takes this weird hair in little clumps out of his pocket and sticks it on around his head when no one's looking.

"What do you think she's gonna do, Euless? Injure somebody with her shirttail?"

"Make her put it in, or get another batter."

"Play ball!" everybody yells.

It's very embarrassing.

So I get to stand there stuffing all of that itchy uniform inside my belt, and finally I can bat.

Then I look out at Acie Barker.

Oh, Katie Dee— I had never really seen him before. Never really looked at him. But when you are there by yourself you see the best pitcher in the county—you know that he's bigger than anything. And he's on top of a mountain looking down at you in that gray uniform all trimmed in red, with "Cedar Hill" stitched down his chest that really does look as wide as I am tall—he's standing there like that, and all you have is a bat.

"Playball!"

"Comebaby!"

He winds up and kicks his leg; I can hear him grunt.

"Uuuh!"

The ball roars by like a white train; pow, it's a shotgun blast into the catcher's mitt.

"Steerrike!"

"Attaboy attaboy attaboy he can't hit he can't hit!"

I want to get mad and tell the catcher that I'm not a "he," but, it's not like he's real easy to talk to at that point. You know?

He almost steps on me when he jumps up to throw the ball back.

It's all so bizarre. I want more than anything not to be there. I have to wear this plastic helmet, and the edge of it cuts into the skin behind my ears, and the inside of it smells like the rubber mats we used to have to sleep on at school.

This time I'm just going to swing. See it and swing, see it

and swing.

No time to watch it, it's going too fast. See it and swing.

He kicks again and throws—

"Swing batter swing batter swing batter—"

There it is!

"Steerike!"

Too fast. It's in that glove by the time I swing. I can't even see it, it's so fast. It scares me, like it's exploding all around me, and I'm just trying to keep it away.

Mr. Caldwell is yelling at me now. Great, just what I need. He's in a line with bunch of other farmers that live out by us. They're all behind the backstop, fingers sticking through the wire. It's like a row of tarantulas had got up there just that high on the wire, moving their brown legs open and closed on the backstop netting. Mr. Caldwell waves me over. "You're trying to kill it," he whispers. "Don't do that. Don't try to kill it. Just meet it. Just meet it."

All I can do is shrug.

What can you say to people like that?

The next pitch, the ball comes right at me, and I dive out of the way, and of course it breaks over the plate—I guess it does, anyway, because I'm lying on the ground and the catcher is so excited the veins in his neck are bulging out like little blue ropes tying his mask to his chest protector.

"Attababy!"

Useless shakes his head. The pitch is so good even he has to call it. He says "strike" the way maybe a doctor would tell somebody that a new baby is dead.

"Strike three. Batter's out. Change sides."

They cheer, and we don't say anything.

Over at the bench, I'm bending down to get my glove, and I see that Mama is there. She has a big fruit jar full of iced tea.

"Here. Have some."

"I need my bat."

"Don't worry about it. It's just a game."

I drink and start toward the field when Bobby Ruskin stops me. All of the Ruskins look alike. Bobby, Useless, Wendall—they all have these kind of cheekbones, and squinty eyes, it's kind of hard to describe but—well, when Mama saw three of them together for the first time she put her hand on her forehead and said, 'My God, they all look like javelinas!' I guess javelinas are a kind of wild hog. Anyway, that's what they look like.

Bobby looks at me and says:

"You play before, or what?"

"Yeah. I've played."

"What? Softball?"

"Baseball."

"Huh."

That's all he says. Then he turns around and starts playing catch with the infield ball.

I look at Mama then. She screws the iced tea top down harder and stares at Bobby.

Then she turns and walks away.

It just goes on like an everyday game then for a while, two or three innings I guess—until something kind of bad happens. It's one of those things that you don't like to write about, but I said I would tell you everything, and so I guess I should. It's the fourth inning and there's no score. Mainly because Acie Barker is so great nobody can hit him, and our pitcher has Useless Ruskin for an umpire, who calls a strike on everything that Bobby can catch. Except, for a while, it's everything Bobby can just catch sitting down but then as our pitcher gets tireder and tireder it gets to be anything Bobby can catch, kind of lunging.

113

Finally I guess their team gets tired of this.

Their coach walks out on the field; he's between the mound and first base. Our coach goes out, too. When he gets to the chalk line between third and home, he stops. He doesn't have to talk very loud, because no one is saying anything.

"What's the matter?"

Their coach doesn't look at him, but just walks very slowly toward home plate, where Useless has taken his mask off.

"What about trying to call the game fairly, ump?"

Then the fence behind me rattles. I jump out of the way, and trip on one of the aluminum bats lying by the ball bag. Looking back up, I can see this man: he has on a caterpillar truck baseball cap and a t-shirt. One of his arms is as big as both of my legs. His stomach shakes, as it kind of sticks out over the top of the fence. He's looking at the other team's coach.

"What about you gettin' off the field, coach?"

He doesn't seem to yell, but it's one of those voices that seems to come out of a bullhorn, just on its own.

Then it's like popcorn. Like, how there's just the corn, not doing anything. After a while, one of the kernels pops. There it is, big and white, where it never was before and doesn't seem to have any business. And then the little explosions start happening, pop pop pop pop—

Just like that, a bunch of people seem to sprout in their stands.

The man beside me is straddling the fence. He has on reddish boots.

"Get off the field! Now!"

He's glaring across the field; and now there are a lot of people over there standing along the baseline.

Then there is a kind of a knot of people around him, and a lot of soft voices, and grownups putting their arms around each other and nodding. The way they do when it isn't really all right, but they keep telling each other how all right it is.

Nobody says anything on our team. There is kind of a bad feeling in everyone's stomach.

Finally the big man leaves. But out in right field the next inning it's a little spooky. The cheering is different. Everyone takes it very serious now, but you have the feeling we all want to be home. When it's hot, and you know tomorrow is Monday, and it isn't really fun at all. You know, Katie Dee, how sometimes you're supposed to be working, and you are working, but it's more fun than playing? Like Friday morning in math at school—it's math all right, but you know the afternoon is just right there in front of you, so close you can touch it, and it will be a golden Friday afternoon down on the creek, and the next day will be Saturday. Saturday morning, in early November, overcast and kind of cool, with all the weekend still there spreading out in every direction. All of that is in front of you, so math isn't bad. Just like nothing is good on Sunday afternoon, not even play, not even Water Carnival.

Well that's the way sometimes it is playing baseball, especially if a lot of grownups are around.

Standing out in right field I look for the big man with the stomach hanging over the fence, but I don't see him.

I don't see Mama, either. She's probably gone off somewhere. She's always telling me she doesn't like tension. I look for her in the truck, but then I see the truck isn't there, either. I don't know where she's gone.

And then I feel even spookier. I don't know these people. Not really. And I don't even have my mother there. What if there's a fight, a real fight?

I just want to be back out on our farm.

Two more innings go by. I strike out again, but I don't want to talk about that. Mama is still gone. I don't know what's happened to her.

Then I get to thinking. The last inning is coming up. Bobby Ruskin leads off. Then somebody not very good, I don't know his name. Then Marcos. Then me.

I really don't want to bat again in this game.

If all of them make an out I don't have to.

But where is Mama?

I'm thinking about it all the time I'm out there. Good thing nobody hits one to me. (The whole game I only had two balls come to me, and both of them were on the ground. Whew.) But as we go in for our last at-bats I keep looking around, up and down the lines. The people are smoking now, men and women, little trails of cigarette smoke snaking up into the black sky and twisting around the lights around the infield. The women especially look very hard, and they're clapping. We're one run behind—they finally scored so it's one to nothing—and we're all clapping, too, hitting each other on the back. As for me, I don't care. I sit down with my back up against the fence, and I'm just praying: God, don't let me have to bat again. God, don't let me have to bat again.

But how will I get home?

Darryl comes and sits down by me. I wish he'd go away.

"You get on," he says, "and I'll drive you in."

"Right. Like that's really going to happen."

"Hey. You got to believe."

"I just want to go home, Darryl." He shakes his head.

"You get on, I'm gonna drive you in." He shrugs and walks away.

Bobby Ruskin strikes out. The batter that I don't know his name is up now; when he leans over the plate it looks like he's got like polio or something.

"Steerike one!"

116

The pitch is about a foot high, but Useless wants to go home too. You can tell. Cars are starting to pull away. The headlights are going on, all up and down the foul lines. There is the growl of motors, and these huge pickup trucks with guns in the back start edging their way out into the street.

"Yourrouuut!"

The kid walks back, probably happy the ball didn't kill him. Acie Barker is throwing harder now. He's grinning, up there on the mound as the parents stand up in the Cedar Hill stands, and their infielders whip the ball around, yelling all of that stupid stuff they have to yell.

I have to go into the on deck circle. Marcos is up, and there's no way he's going to hit it. I mean, no way. But I have to get a bat I can't swing, and go outside the dugout, and lean on the bat with one knee up and one leg behind me the way they do it in the big leagues. It's kind of eerie there, halfway to the plate. You can hear the cheering louder; the lights glare down on you, and it seems everybody is looking at you, even though they aren't.

The first pitch hits the mitt like a shotgun going off. Acie Barker must be twenty years old, I mean it. It isn't fair. They shouldn't be letting him pitch in this league. You should see him out there. He ought to be in a grown men's league.

Then it happens—whap. Everyone's numb for what seems like a second but it must be shorter. The ball has hit Marcos right below the ribs, and he's down, first on one knee, then on the ground, twisting around like a snake and screaming. Suddenly there are a lot of people running by me, big people, parents and coaches and, I guess, doctors. I'm like a rock stuck in the creek with the water all running by it. I can't see Marcos now. But I do see the big man with the stomach hanging over. He's at the fence again, behind third base. Nobody's looking at him, but I am. He's got a couple of guys beside him now, mean skinny looking guys with cement company caps and cigarettes now in their mouths, now at their sides down by their jeans. He's just glaring, while the knot of people mills around home plate and everybody in the Cedar Hill stands is up on their feet, keeping quiet, watching.

The knot dissolves; it just breaks away, and there is Marcos, grinning now, running down to first base. His face is all covered with sand, like his uniform, and you can see the trails glistening down his cheek where tears had been; but he's running, and our crowd cheers him. So does the Cedar Hill crowd. He's OK.

But I'm up.

Coach runs over from third base. He puts his arm around me. I can smell some kind of after shave lotion, and his face is so close to me that the bill of his cap touches my nose. Coach's voice is low as a tractor motor.

"You want to bat?"

I don't know what to say for a minute. I don't want to bat. I don't want to go out there.

But I can't seem to make myself say anything.

"If you don't want to bat, Sugar, I'll put somebody in for you. You want me to do that?"

Finally my voice comes back.

"Yes. Put somebody in for me."

"Okay. Euless!"

I turn around to go back to the dugout, and just glance at the fence, behind home plate. There are all the loafers, not saying anything, their cigars all going; and there's Mama.

She has my bat.

I walk over to her.

"Here it is, if you want to use it," she says.

I don't say anything; she lifts up the mesh wire, and slides the bat under it.

I go back over to coach, and catch up with him before he gets to Useless.

"I think I want to bat."

Coach looks down at me; so does Useless, little BB eyes squinting down from behind the umpire's mask.

"You sure?"

"Yeah."

Then Darryl yells from the on deck circle.

"Get on. I'll drive you in."

Right, Darryl.

"Let her bat," says coach to Useless.

"Play ball!" Useless yells.

And everybody starts cheering.

I'm getting sand on my hands.

There's this other hand on my shoulder; it's Darryl, and he shouldn't be there. He should be in the on deck circle.

"Bunt," he whispers.

"What?"

"Bunt. You bunt, you make it. Bunt down first, don't bunt down third. Look where the first baseman is; just look at him. He's way back in the outfield. He thinks the game's over. Bunt. I can hit this chump. I'll drive you in."

He's right; the first baseman is behind Marcos, kind of teasing him, tagging him with an imaginary ball. Marcos looks scared to death now. He's maybe six inches from the bag, rubbing his side where the ball hit him.

"OK. I'll bunt."

"I'm gonna drive you in man."

I don't tell him I'm not any "man," because I'm thinking about bunting. Acie Barker rubs up the ball. He's taller than ever, and sweat glistens all over what you can see of him that isn't uniform. He wants to get it over with. They all do, all of the infielders. They've got their hands cupped around their mouths, and they're screaming. The people in the stands are waving their baseball caps and straw cowboy hats.

Useless steps out in front of the plate, turns around so that his behind is toward Acie Barker, and wipes sand off the plate with a little miniature broom that he's got.

"Play ball."

My bat feels good. It's slender, and my hands can get around it. It's nicked on the meat end where, sometimes at home, I throw rocks up and hit them toward the pecan trees bordering the creek. I can't get it around to hit the fastball. It's too fast. I know that already. But if I can just get squared around, and push it up toward first base.

It might work.

He kicks so high that I can't see his face.

Then—it's just a blur and it's coming right at my head. I know it's going to hit me, Katie Dee. I still see it coming at me, sometimes at night in a dream. And then I try to move and I can't. I'm paralyzed.

Somehow—I don't know how—I manage to fall down, rump first. It can't have missed me by much. All I know is the catcher lunges to catch, and almost steps on me. Where it hits the mitt, my head was. Everything is quiet for just an instant. I'm kind of sprawled in the sand with the catcher straddling me. The big man, down the third base line, is out on the field then. I just feel him there; and I'm not surprised when that voice comes:

"Throw it at the plate, you little jerk!"

They just kind of hang there over the field, there in the hot night. I know there's going to be a fight. You can hear both stands vibrating as people, one at a time, one row at a time then—all of them stand up.

"Hit it, Katie."

It's Mama.

I look around. I guess everybody does. She's just standing there behind home plate, between Mr. Caldwell and the other loafers. She has on her scarf, and dark glasses. She puts her hand up and takes the glasses off. She doesn't talk loud, but somehow you can hear her as well as you can hear the big man:

"Hit it, Katie."

Then Mr. Caldwell yells:

"Don't try and kill it; just meet it."

And then everyone starts yelling.

"Hit it, Katie!"

"Get her out! Get her out!"

And Acie Barker gets back on the mound.

I'm saying to myself:

"Just see it; just see it; get the bat on it; bunt it, bunt it bunt it see it see it see it…

He kicks again and grunts and there it is. It's just there, Katie Dee. I can't explain it. It's kind of low and outside, and for a minute, about two thirds of way between the plate and the mound—right there—it just freezes. I can see it better, and clearer, than anything I've ever seen. I can count the stitches on it. It's waiting there, hanging there, like it was a picture of a ball someone had put up out in the middle of the field.

I swing at it as hard as I can.

The bat bends. Sometimes that happens. You swing harder than you've ever swung, and the bat seems six inches thick with meat at the end and the ball and the bat are one thing and the bat just bends in your hands like rubber.

Whack.

The ball arches, curving over the first baseman's head bending back foul, foul, back toward the right field line. It's going foul. It's going foul.

Then a little puff of chalk dust floats up. The ball disappears, rolling back toward the grandstand.

"Fair ball! Go! Go! Go! Go!"

Somewhere between home and first I guess I must have knocked the batting helmet off my head; because I can feel my braid flying as I kick the bag and go almost into right field making the turn. The rightfielder still has his back to me; he's still chasing it. In the corner of my eye our coach, over at third, is jumping up and down, making huge circles with his arm. Everyone else is jumping up and down, too. There's just this roar.

"Go Katie! Go Katie Go Katie Go Katie—"

You can only see glimpses of the people in both stands waving their arms and bouncing on the boards but mostly you have to think about running as fast as you've ever run, because he's got the ball now and I'm around second. The sand is loose out there; it doesn't matter. I know I've got it. I know by the third baseman's eyes as he looks up at the throw coming at him. I'm closer to him than the ball is. I slide on my stomach, skidding ten feet on that red sand and getting it in my mouth, but my hand is on the canvas base when I hear the ball thud into the glove above me.

"Safe!"

"Yes!"

Everyone's yelling. The third baseman walks toward the mound and throws the ball to Acie Barker, while I try to stand up. The coach is right by me, helping me. There's a bunch of people over by the fence ten feet away, yelling and throwing their fists and hats in the air. I try not to look at them. You have to walk around a little. There's sand caked on the front of my uniform, and it feels like there's no more skin on my navel and knees.

Mama is sitting in the truck again. It's out behind me, behind a row of cars down the left field line. You can just see her face behind the windshield, but it's hard to tell if she's smiling or not.

It takes a while to get everybody quieted down.

The game is tied, and I'm the winning run.

Don't get picked off; don't get picked off; don't get picked off...

There goes Darryl, walking to the plate like he hasn't got a care in the world. He's struck out twice already and he hasn't come close to the ball. But he's walking up to the plate like he's Mickey Mantle or somebody. Just sauntering, taking his time.

"C'mon Darryl! C'mon Darryl!"

Everybody's yelling. Either at Darryl or at Acie. Nobody's sitting down. Some of the cars that had begun to back out are stuck now, halfway out in the street. The people in them or standing up, in and out of their cars. Horns keep going off, either telling other cars to move, or just cheering for Darryl.

Who looks, of course, like he's in a dream world.

"OK Darryl. Get one for us pal."

I glance over at coach, who is clapping and talking to Darryl.

And rubbing his hand across his belt.

His hand across his belt.

"C'mon Darryl Hey Darryl. Just one swing is all it takes."

His hand across his belt again.

The squeeze play.

"C'mon Darryl. Just takes one."

Darryl, bat on the shoulder, stares out toward the bandstand. He hasn't looked at coach once.

I'm still standing right on top of the base. The pitcher, right on top of the mound, keeps rubbing up the ball. You can see sweat shining on him. It's very hot. His uniform looks like he has just gone swimming in it, and sweat is all over his face and neck.

I know I shouldn't talk, but...

"Coach..."

It's all right, Katie," he says, quietly. "Just keep your head in the game."

"Play ball!" Useless yells.

"Get your lead, Katie."

"Coach, I..."

"Get your lead. Keep your head in the game."

"Come baby come baby come baby..."

"Play ball!"

Darryl whacks the bat on the plate twice. Then he steps up; he's staring out at the pitcher, just staring at him, cold. He hasn't looked at coach once. I know what he's thinking. He's gonna knock the ball over the fence. Only he can't, because he can't hit Acie Barker. He can't even come close.

Coach rubs his hand over his belt.

Why doesn't he call time out?

When Acie Barker lifts his leg, when he starts his big kick, I have to take off. If Darryl doesn't bunt the ball, then there I am, about halfway to home plate, a human dork. Darryl, look! Look, Darryl!

Somehow, time out is called. It's their coach. He walks toward the mound, yelling something to the first baseman. I can't make out what he's yelling.

Darryl keeps staring at the bandstand.

"Play ball!"

Then Acie Barker nods at the catcher, and begins his windup. He can't stop now.

Maybe I can beat the ball to the plate. Maybe I'm that fast. I just take off, Katie Dee, and it's like a dream, or a nightmare, when you're running in jelly. You can't get up enough speed. Not quick enough. You're bending low, driving your legs, but it's never fast enough. Acie sees me when I'm a third of the way to the plate, but he's coming over the top now with the ball and releasing it—all I can do is bore straight ahead, oh Katie, they're still too far in front of me, the catcher standing up waiting for the ball and Useless crouching to the side—I'll never make it...

And Darryl bunts the ball.

It's a beautiful soft bunt, like he's just flicked his bat and wished it out in front of the plate, rolling, a little to the side, skidding along on sand and the first baseman diving toward it; out of the corner of my eye I see him scoop it up and throw it underhand but I'm diving at the plate...

"GO KATIE GO KATIE GO KATIE GO KATIE..."

I crash into the catcher's legs, those plastic shinguards, and then everything crashes down on me, if you can imagine a sack of feed, more than a hundred pounds, just whamming down on you. I don't know what's happening. The metal catcher's mask is rammed into the back of my neck; someone's pounding my back with the ball, the catcher I guess, and there's so much sand in my face that I can't open my eyes. Finally I spit it out, and can get my head raised.

There's Useless, crouched right in front of me, not moving, as though he's inspecting the dirt.

There's no sound at all, I swear.

Then his arms fly out to his side.

"Safe! She's safe!"

The catcher jumps up and throws the mask down. It bounces off the plate. But I lose sight of everything then, because people are grabbing me. It was so quiet for just an instant, and now—I can't even describe the noise. Everybody wants to tell me how great I am and—you know, that stuff.

I'm not going to tell you about the rest of it. Just—people know me now, and that's nice. Just one more thing. We're all getting into the back of the pickup to go to the Dairy Queen, and I go over to Darryl.

"Did you see that sign, Darryl, or did you just bunt when you saw me coming?"

He kind of shrugs.

"You didn't see it; you didn't see it, did you? You were looking out at the bandstand. Admit it—you didn't see it!"

Then he kind of grins.

"I tell you I'm gonna knock you in—and that's what I did, didn't I?"

"But you didn't see the sign!"

He just says:

"Shoot."

And walks off.

Boys.

Forever yours,

Katie Haw

The Night the Gin
Burned Down

The Night the Gin Burned Down

August 6, 1967
Midlothian, Texas

Dear Katie Dee,

You need to have something to look forward to, Katie Dee, just to get you through the bad stuff. Like church in the hot summer, when you have to dress up, and it's been a bad week anyway because you've had to hoe corn all week. Church can be kind of hard anyway, especially when you have to be Act-O-Light, Brother Jenkins leads prayer that day, and you don't have anything to color. But when you know that the corn has just come up, and you've got acres and acres of the stuff that you've just got to start hoeing the next day—well, that's even worse.

So, what I had to look forward to that Sunday morning was eating lunch over at Grandma's and staying the whole afternoon and spending the night, and getting her to tell the story of the night the gin burned down. It's the best story I've ever heard; I'll tell it to you a little later, and I'll tell you how Grandma tells it, and the things she does when she tells it.

Church was first, though. Being Act-O-Light is when you and Matthew Kerns have to put on choir robes—you two being the only ones big enough to be able to do it and little enough to still be cute—and walk down the aisles with these long gold rods that burn at the ends and perform an Act-Of-Light, which is lighting all the candles that are up in front of the flowers and behind the preacher.

Except you can barely do it in the summer, because they have the air conditioner on, and the air blows out of the vents up by the spotlights in the ceiling and puts out the candle as soon as you light it. You have to keep *lighting* it and *lighting* it and *lighting* it and Matthew Kerns just standing there the whole time because he's already lit his that is on the other side where the vent doesn't blow, but him being the Sunday School Superintendent's kid you can't make him change sides.

So anyway I knew it would be a hard morning even when Mama and I showed up at nine to fellowship. Fellowship means when the grownup women have coffee in the church kitchen and the grownup men stand outside and smoke. I like to watch the men from the kitchen window.

Beyond the church is the cemetery, where we're all buried, and beyond that Long Branch Creek. But just on this side of the cemetery there are some huge cedar trees and that's where the men stand. James Parker and Chuggy Conroy and Dan Metzenbaum and Floyd Thompson and Bob Metzenbaum and Hoss Prothro and Jesse Peters—they kind of root themselves down like *they* were cedar trees and stand staring out past the creek with their hands on their belts, not saying very much, just nodding every now and then like everything was happening the way they thought it would.

So this Sunday we fellowshipped, then we went in to the sanctuary and sang. It was an Easter song, even though this was August. We sing it a lot because Bob Metzenbaum likes it. It begins with all of us singing, real low and quiet like we're depressed:

Low in the grave he lay Jesus my Savior... Waiting the coming day.. Jesus my Lord.

And then there is a kind of pause, and all the men with the bass voices go down real low, like they're getting him out of the grave, and sing:

Up from the grave he arose...

Once they have done the 'Up from the grave he a...' part, Bob Metzenbaum, who has the deepest bass voice of anybody, comes in from the very back pew with another '*Up from the grave he a*', kind of on his own, so while everybody else is just holding out *rooooooose*, he's climbing to get up with us with the same deep words, like a bass echo from the back of the church. Then we just get higher and higher all together, and there's no timing on the '*rose*'s so you can just hold them out as long as you want to.

He aroooooooooooose! He aroooooooooooooooose!
Hal-a-lew-yah, Chriiiiiiist arooose.

Then we do another verse, which is kind of the same thing. Then we go to Sunday school.

Bob Tucker is our teacher. Today was stewardship Sunday. Stewardship in our church is another word for money. He asked us if a rich man could enter into the kingdom of heaven and nobody said anything so he said we should all read in the bible about the camel and the eye of the needle. We did. He asked us what that meant to us, and nobody still said anything, and it was stupid to just sit there, so I said well I guess that means rich people can't go to heaven but he just shook his head and said that was what I thought because I didn't know Hebrew.

Which I don't.

And if I did, he said, I'd know that the 'eye of the needle' was in Jerusalem and was a kind of an arch that if a camel would bend down he could go under it, so that left me a little confused because does that mean you can be rich and get into heaven if you just bend down a little going in, because that doesn't sound like much trouble? He said there was nothing wrong with being rich, only there was if you loved your money more than the Lord but if you loved the Lord more than your money then you could have as much of it as you wanted. Money, I mean.

Then we went back to church and had Holy Communion.

Which was a disaster.

There was Matthew Kerns—why *he* was sitting with us I don't know—then me, then Mama. The little flat plate with the tiny crackers came by, no problem. But then there was the big deep silver platter. It had maybe fifty of those glasses with Jesus' Blood that had been Welch's Grape Juice before it got changed by a miracle, I guess somewhere down the hall between the adults' Sunday School Class and the kitchen.

You're supposed to take one out with the tips of your fingers, drink it, and put it back. But this time, when the plate got to me, all of the little glasses were empty. Every one of them. I mean, not 'empty' all the way but so that you could see somebody had drunk out of them and there was only a film of Blood in the bottom of each one.

I had it there, the whole tray, balanced on my knees, passing my hand over it, trying to figure out what to do.

It felt like everybody was looking at me.

It especially felt like Hoss Prothro was looking at me. He was waiting at the end of the aisle to get the tray back, probably knowing that George Henry Simpson and Clifton Dale Mackey had already gotten ahead of him in the center and right aisles, and were probably going to finish first.

So what could I do? I just took an empty glass, put it up to my lips, threw my head back, kind of licked my lips, said 'ahhh,' like it had been good, put the glass back, and passed the tray on down to Matthew Kerns.

He wouldn't take it.

"You didn't get one," he said.

I could have killed him.

"Take it," I whispered, kind of hissing, and jabbing the tray at him so that the glasses rattled.

"Take it."

But he just looked past me and at Mama.

"She didn't get one."

"Take it," I kept saying.

"The one she drank out of was empty. I saw it."

"Matthew you take this tray, you SuperDork!"

"Katherine Marie..."

"Mama make him take it!"

"Take the tray, Matthew."

"But they're all empty! Katie was faking!"

I don't know how long this would have gone on if Clifton Dale Mackey hadn't come over to help us. He still had some full glasses in his tray, and Matthew took one. I didn't though, even though he was glaring at me and I was glaring at him and Mommy was breathing deep like she does when she's mad at me and can't say anything because of all the people around. It does worry me because if I die between now and the next time we Commune with the Holy Spirit I won't be blessed; but I wasn't going to give in to Matthew Kerns.

Mama had some kind of mad things to tell me about all that, riding over to Grandma's. But in the end, she did agree that Matthew Kerns was kind of a Superdork, and that a lot of it was his fault.

Then it was all OK, and we could talk about Grandma.

Mama always smiled when she talked about Grandma, and her stories.

"Your grandma, Katie, is a natural story teller. She's one of those storytellers who sets out to tell you one story, and then gets sidetracked on a dozen others, and never gets around to the one you're expecting. And you don't mind, because you've had such a good time listening to all of the others. None of which were probably true in the first place. That's your grandma. She's an artist. She taught school for thirty two years in Midlothian. Third grade. Some of the meanest little boys in the world. Boys who are now men and in jail, and should have been in jail even then. Tough boys. But if you go to the filling station or the cement plant even now and ask those men—the ones that aren't behind bars—how much they hated school, they'll smile and spit and say they hated all of it except that third grade. And then they'll tell you how they still remember *The Bears of Blue River*, or some other book your grandmother read them, or some story she told them."

Or the story of The Night the Gin Burned Down.

I was starved when we got to her house. I never eat any cereal in the morning when we're having lunch there. Floyd Thompson and his wife and Jesse Peters and his wife had been invited to eat with us; they don't have any kids so I got to eat at the main table. It was one of those meals like at Thanksgiving.

Mama says it is an art to have conversation at meals. She says the French do it the best (I don't know how she knows that), and the key to it is wit. We do it pretty well at Grandma's, too.

"Norma, this is just wonderful. Floyd did you get some beans?"

"No, I didn't."

"Pass Floyd the beans."

"There you are."

"Thank you."

"Who needs a roll?"

"These rolls are out of this world."

"I like those cornbread sticks."

"Which way are those going?"

"Are they going around this way? Oh I'm sorry I passed the pickles the other way."

"Could you hand the potatoes down?"

"There you go: watch out, that's hot."

"I have an extra spoon here."

"That goes in the grits."

"Which way is the chicken going?"

"This way I think."

"No, I've had some."

"What I need are the potatoes."

"You didn't get any potatoes?"

"Ooooohhh, will you look at that? She's bringing in the corn!"

"Now—what I need to know is, where do you expect me to put that?"

"Ha ha ha. Ha ha ha."

"I've only got so much room you know."

"You're one to talk, I've already taken off my belt!"

"Ha ha ha. Ha ha ha."

"Where is the butter?"

"It's right here in front of me. Who needs dark meat?"

"Is there any more of that?"

"There sure is."

"Could you pass it around? Watch out—that's hot."

"Oooohh these roastin' ears are just right. I hate them when they get too tough."

"Did you get any fried okra?"

"I don't believe I got the okra."

"Oh. Here, it's stopped in front of me. Let me get it going again."

"Did that okra come from your garden? It's so crisp and good the way you fry it."

"Isn't it good?"

"It's not as good as these tomatoes."

"Do you know we have not had one tomato this year."

"Why not? Would you pass the chicken please?"

"I don't know. Who has the butter?"

"Do you know what? I didn't get any of that ambrosia!"

And on and on like that, with lots of wit like the French do, until Grandma always says: "Now. Who's ready for pie?"

For some reason after lunch I usually feel a little sleepy, so I go upstairs and get my special pallet. It's in a little room that's kind of under the roof in the spare bedroom. That's my favorite place in Grandma's house. It belongs to me, kind of. There are some toys in there that I used to play with, and the broken cookie jar of the little boy with the finger in his nose, and Grandpa's twenty-two rifle.

Anyway, the day I'm telling you about, I got my pallet and lay down in the corner of the bedroom. All around that corner there are stacks of magazines. *Life* magazine, mostly, and *The National Geographic*. I bet Grandma has the world's biggest collection of *The National Geographic*. I like looking through them, especially the real old ones, to see the car advertisements, and the way the women's dresses must have looked in 1930, or whenever the particular magazine I'm looking through is from.

I like to pull a lot of stacks of magazines around the very corner of the room, and spread my pallets out, and take a nap.

When I come downstairs Grandma always acts surprised,

like she didn't know where I was.

I think she did all along, but is just making me feel good.

It was warm in the room, and I could just hear the grownups talking downstairs.

I went to sleep.

* * *

This time, when I woke up, Grandma surprised me. She was in the room, going through a closet. It was five in the afternoon, and the sunlight was all golden coming through the window. You could see dust floating in the air.

She smiled at me.

"So there you are, little rabbit."

"Did I surprise you, Grandma?"

"Certainly did. Startled me out of my wits."

"What are you doing?"

"I'm going through this old armoire. It must be a year since I've been up here. Here. Look."

She showed me an old picture. It showed a rich looking man in a suit. It looked like old pictures always looked. The man was not smiling.

"Your great great grandfather, Sam Hawkins. The river boat captain."

"River boat?"

"Yes. He ran a river boat in Louisiana. Near Coushatta. Your great great grandmother—she was an Armistead—fell in love with him."

"Was she pretty?"

"Oh, beautiful. There are pictures of her around here, somewhere. She was a southern belle, and lived in a great plantation near Coushatta. The liveoaks made a pathway down to the river. I've often wondered if she drove with her riverboat captain down that liveoak lane in a carriage. But at any rate he won her heart and stole her away. They came to Texas. To Midlothian, actually, and he built a house near where this one stands now. You remember the old well down between here and the creek?"

"Yes."

"There. That was where the house stood. She had eleven children, and, when she was thirty six, she died. Well, Sam wanted to build her a splendid tomb. So he hired an above ground tomb sculpted in Metairie Cemetery, down in New Orleans."

"That must have cost a lot."

"Oh, I'm sure it did. But he had inherited a great deal of the Armistead cotton money, and so cost was no object. So he planned to take the body by train over to Louisiana, and then down the Mississippi River to New Orleans."

"Planned?"

"Well, things didn't go quite so quickly in those days. So the body had to lie in state on the porch of the farmhouse for something like two months."

"Oh gross!"

"Yes, it caused somewhat of a stir. The workers were uneasy."

"That's weird. And gross. She was just... there?"

"She was just there, for two months. Then the tomb was ready. So Sam and the corpse of his wife went down to New Orleans on a train and a riverboat."

"Did he stay in the same room with her?"

"I don't know, dear. But at any rate, after some days they arrived in New Orleans, and he went to Metairie Cemetery to view the tomb. He didn't like it."

"What?"

"No, for some reason he didn't like it. So he contracted for a different tomb, and from a different sculptor. Then he put his wife's body in a riverboat going upstream, and brought her back here, to Midlothian."

I couldn't believe that.

"Grandma..."

"No, it's true. This all happened in around 1880, and there are accounts of it in the local papers. He was not a popular figure around the town."

"I guess not. How long did it take to get the other grave ready?"

"Nine months."

"Oh no. And so she..."

"Yes, she stayed on the front porch."

"I don't believe that."

"Nevertheless, it happened. The tales are, of course, that on moonlit nights you could see her ghost wandering among the trees down by Long Branch."

"Oh Grandma."

She just smiled.

It's hard to describe Grandma. She's like a lot of grandmas, I guess. There are big grandmas and little grandmas. Mine is a little grandma. Her hair is not snow white, but brown. There are pictures of her a long time ago, and she had to wear her hair in a big bun; but now her hair is short. The backs of her hands are brown splotched and her neck is wrinkled; that doesn't sound very pretty, but I think my grandma is beautiful. There's something about her eyes, and the way they sparkle when she looks at you. And her smile. If Grandma has wrinkles, it's mostly because she has smiled so much in her life, I think.

"I believe it all, Grandma. Except the ghost part."

"No. That's hard to believe, I guess."

"I used to believe in ghosts, when I was little. It took me a while to grow out of it, and learn that they don't exist."

She just nodded, and looked like she was thinking.

"They don't exist, do they?"

"Not usually, Katie."

"Not usually?"

"No."

"You mean they exist sometimes?"

She just shrugged, and had that look old people have, when you think they know a lot that you don't know. It's a look that makes you feel like you were little, and very young, like three, and not old, like ten.

"You mean they exist sometimes?"

"A lot of things exist sometimes."

"Have you ever seen a ghost?"

She was quiet for a while. The sun was real low in the sky. Queen the collie dog had been lying on the back porch all day, and was beginning to bark now. We would have to feed her.

"Katie, when World War II broke out, your mother was only ten years old but your Uncle Owen was twenty-one. So of course they took him immediately. They also took Miller Walker."

"Who was he?"

"Miller was Owen's best friend. Oh, the two of them had grown up together. They were inseparable. Owen and Miller had roamed these creeks together as boys, and hunted together, and worked on the thresher crews all over four counties."

"At any rate, within six months after Pearl Harbor they were both overseas. We didn't know where. There were practically no letters. But one day in November of 1942—I shall always remember it—I had come up here, and was cleaning. It was a Saturday, about this time of day. It had gotten so dusty; the wind was just howling outside, and with the plowed fields you could never keep the dirt out. I saw someone move in the doorway and wondered who could have come up the stairs. Your grandfather was still alive then, but I knew him to be plowing over at the farm where you and your mother live now. It was Miller. It surprised me—shocked me, I should say, because I knew he was overseas, and there seemed no way he could have gotten home. His uniform shone, the buttons polished, the brown shoes so shiny... I was so delighted to see him that I started to run to him, but he just shook his head and smiled. 'Owen will come home. Don't worry. Owen will come home.' And then he left. I went immediately to his house and asked his mother—Clarice Walker was still teaching at that time—I asked her if she had heard from him, or if he had gone by there first."

"What did she say?"

Grandma was quiet for a time, just looking out of the window.

Then she said, "She had been crying. They had gotten word only an hour before. Miller's transport had been sunk by a German submarine, all lost at sea."

For a while I didn't say anything. There wasn't much to say, I guess. Grandma went on:

"And your Uncle Owen did come home, of course. He was shot while leading a patrol, but he survived. And he came home. And I never spoke of seeing Miller. Not until today. Isn't that strange?"

After a while, I asked:

"Could you have dreamed it?"

Then she just smiled a little grandma smile:

"No. No, Katie, I didn't dream it."

"Then... I wish there had been a Miller Walker for Daddy."

She got up, and walked over to where I was sitting on my pallet, and stroked my hair.

"I do, too, darling. I do, too."

"Do you think that Miller Walker and Daddy would have been good friends?"

"I think that Miller Walker and your daddy *are* good friends. And I believe that with all my heart. Now: how does ice cream sound?"

"It sounds good."

"Then let's go down and make some."

"After that will you tell me the story of The Night the Gin Burned Down?"

"We'll see."

That always means 'yes' when grandma says it.

"And will you tell it the long way?"

"We'll see."

So we went downstairs.

And I thought, all the time we were cranking the ice cream freezer, that Mama was right. Grandma was a natural story-teller. Anything—a walnut luck charm that had belonged to Grandpa, or a red and blue handkerchief that the two of them had gotten when they went to the Texas Centennial, or a dog barking in the field at night, or an old chimney standing in a burned out house—anything would start a story, as though the whole world, that you think sometimes is so boring and nothing ever happens in it—that the whole world is one story after another, if you have a grandma who's a storyteller.

And tonight she was going to tell the story of the The Night the Gin Burned Down.

And sometime, Katie Dee, I'll tell it to you.

Always,

Katie Haw

142

Second Best Friend

Second Best Friend

Dear Katie Dee,

We finished picking corn at about 7:00. It wasn't quite dark yet, but the days are getting shorter. We were tired and so was Mr. Burton, and we still had to unload one wagon load into the bin at the barn. That was worse than anything. All day I had been driving the tractor, pulling the wagon around the field to wherever Mr. Burton happened to stop the cornpicker with a full hopper of corn. Then there was working the wagon around ever so easy, in first gear, ramming the clutch in and easing it out again, so that the tractor jumped and shook and roared and eased forward, and the trailer rolled up to the picker just inches away from those huge orange fan belt gears that looked like two foot round clocks and that, if I ever got too close, would just shear right off the combine with an awful grating of metal and yelling of Mr. Burton.

Not to mention Mama.

So that, by seven, when, working with those two big scoops, we got the last of the wagon emptied into the bin, all I wanted was a real bath.

"I'll unhitch the trailer, Katie. You put the tractor in the shed."

"All right."

"Don't just throttle it down until it dies, now. Push in the ignition button, too. We don't want a dead battery tomorrow; we've got too much field left to do."

145

"All right."

I jumped down from the trailer, looking up at that door of the bin and wondering how we could have thrown those scoopfuls of corn up there. My palms were beginning to blister, and my back and shoulders felt worse than they do when you do exercises, and haven't done them in a long time, and get up in the morning the next day.

"I'll stay down here at the barn and get the sheep put up."

"All right, Mama!"

"Then what do you say we go to the movies?"

"What?"

Because I couldn't believe I had heard her right.

"I said, 'let's go to the movies.'"

"Yes! Yes, yes!"

"All right, then. Get moving."

And I did, driving the tractor back up to the house in road gear (when it should have been in third), and wondering what was showing, and if I could take Gretchen. I didn't even know what was playing at the Ellis—because this late, on a fall Saturday night, she *had* to mean the Ellis Drive In Theater.

I got the tractor put away and walked into the house, not the back way but out on the front porch. You could look through the porch screen and see the whole farm stretching up to the east. There was a harvestmoon bigger than a pumpkin hanging just above the far hedgerow; and between me and the moon was half of the land in deadripe corn, corn with dried ears hanging and ready to snap off, and the other half, closer to the house, in corn the way it looks when it's been run through the picker.

I knew there was a Waxahachie paper on the porch swing. I had almost gone to sleep reading after lunch. There is nothing harder than going back to combining in the middle of the day when all you want to do is lie on the swing and read the paper.

146

The east screen of the Ellis had *Love in the Afternoon*. The west screen had *It Came From Beneath the Sea*.

"Yes!"

First feature: 8:00.

The front screen door banged shut.

"Mama!"

"Yes!"

"Can I take Gretchen?"

"If she wants to go. It's short notice."

She was right. We didn't have much time, because it was already seven o'clock; but of course Gretchen just lived two miles away on the Waxahachie highway so we could get her as we drove past.

I called her.

Please don't let her be spending the night with Emily Hall.

"Gretchen!"

"Hi Katie."

"Mama and I are going to the movies. Want to go?"

"Yes! Oh yes, oh yes oh thank you! I am *so* bored here. You don't *know* how bored I am!"

"You know what's showing?"

"I don't *care* what's showing, Katie. Anything could be showing."

"It Came From Beneath the Sea!"

"*Yes! Yes! Yes!*"

"We'll pick you up as soon as we can get there."

So of course I had to change clothes and bathe, which I did with two kettles on the front burners of the stove. Mama said she would wait to bathe until she got home, but it was getting cold and she might just skip it.

I thought about skipping it. But when you're really itchy there's nothing like putting two pans of water on the stove, heat-ing them up, pouring them smoking and scalding into the tub, then letting just enough cold in so that it's knife-blade hot.

Then I had to get the truck ready, which for a drive-in movie meant tool-shed quilts. Tool-shed quilts are ones that you sleep out on. They're always folded in a special old trunk, and you never sleep on them in the regular way. They're the blankets that, when you and a friend say, 'Mama, can we sleep out to-night?', your mama says, "Well, all right, get that old thick quilt out of the trunk in the toolshed."

You need a regular bed quilt and a toolshed quilt.

I got it out and it smelled all musty. I laid it over my arm and lugged it out to the truck, and then unfolded it and spread it just right, making sure there were no sticks or twigs under it. Then I got three big pillows and rammed them up against the cab end of the truck bed.

Twenty minutes to go when Mama came out.

Just right.

"Hold in."

"All right."

Why do parents, when you ride in the back of the pick up truck and it's on the farm to market road, which is asphalt, and you're going fifty miles an hour and the wind is hurricaning by so loud you have to scream right in somebody's ear just to make a whisper—why do parents always tell you then to hold in?

Like, do they think you're going to jump out?

I didn't jump out, neither on the bouncy gravel road which kills your bottom and back and that little bone right at the base of your spinal cord; nor on the real road, but just lay flat as I could and watched the trees go by all nomoreleaved, handlimbholding together where they had grown together above the road, the stars coming out spotted among the branches.

When we turned on to the farm-to-market road I got to see

the moon again. It was getting yellow now but was still so big and round that you never remembered the moon could be that big.

The truck sped up; it was getting colder now, but the quilts made it all right.

Gretchen has two dogs, Furrier and Ives. I don't know what kind of dogs they are, except they're big. Furrier, when he jumped up on the truck, could get his paws over the side of the truck bed. Each one of his paws was about as big as a toad frog.

"Hi Katie!"

"Hi Gretchen!"

"Furrier get down from there!"

He didn't, of course, but just kept trying to lick me, which I had to pretend I liked. Slobber pant tongue out slobber pant—

"Furrier! Bad dog! Get away from there!"

"It's all right, Gretchen. I like Furrier."

I hate Furrier.

Slobber pant tongue out slobber pant *bark bark bark bark* slobber pant claws scratching on the truck side...

"Furrier! You are a bad dog..."

While Gretchen's mother had to thank my mama for taking Gretchen and Gretchen has money to pay for the movie and money for one hotdog and not two and oh no, Gretchen is our guest for the evening and blah blah blah blah blah.

Slobber pant slobber pant slobber pant

Finally we pulled away. We had fifteen minutes.

Her house was two hundred yards behind us now, and you could still hear Furrier howling.

It's hard to talk when the truck is going fast, so mostly we just lay side by side, looking up, watching for meteors—we have an understood meteor contest, it's who can see the meteor first, but both of us have to see it before it burns out or it doesn't count.

Once Gretchen yelled:

"What's *It Came from Beneath the Sea* about?"

"Giant octopus."

And that's all we said on the ride in.

You have to drive through downtown Waxahachie to get to the Ellis. It seems like a long way when you're almost late for a movie; but you go past I guess a hundred or more of these old, old houses with railings and banisters that have been carved to look like curly-Q french fries. It was really dark now; people had turned on their porch lights, and back in the drive ways behind the yard trees and shrubbery you could see someone every now and then out in the garage cleaning the barbeque grill.

Gretchen and I were sitting up now, shoulder to shoulder, backs against the cab.

"How does the octopus get to be a giant?"

"H-bomb."

"What do you want to be when you grow up?"

"An archeologist."

"I want to be an ichthyologist."

"What's that?"

"Someone who studies the South Pole."

"Why would you want to do that?"

"I don't know. I've always liked the South Pole. I like to look at it on the globe at school. It's so white."

"Would you make much money?"

"I don't care. As long as I get to go to the South Pole and explore there."

"If I can't be an archeologist I might want to be a basketball player."

"It's good to have more than one thing to do. In case the first one isn't as good as you thought. If I can't be an ichthyologist I want to be the person who paints the boxcars on trains."

"That would be neat. You could paint them all kinds of designs."

"They might make you paint them a certain way, though."

"Yeah. Most trains are kind of boring when you look at them. You should stick to being an ichthyologist."

There was a line of cars at the Ellis, but they had double booths so you could pay at the left window or the right window. The back of the drive-in was huge; it must have been fifty feet high, or a hundred feet, and on it were giant buzzing neon rods that crackled and zapped mosquitoes and that spelled out in green red orange and purple the word 'Ellis'.

After you paid you drove around a high, sheet metal fence and then, when you turned, you could see they were showing previews. The playground below the screen, still lighted, looked like a pinball machine and fifty or so little kids were the pinballs, careening around and screaming, doing everything on the swing sets except actually getting in the swings and swinging; and they looked funny because right above them in the movie preview this guy dressed like Robin Hood (but not really Robin Hood I don't think because he had on black Robin Hood clothes instead of green Robin Hood clothes) was being chased by some knights through all the rooms of a castle. Finally he grabbed a torch—there were lots of torches burning in the castle—and threw it at the knights, but it didn't do any good, and they just kept on chasing him. This was on the west screen. The east screen preview was boring.

You could barely hear the words and music from either screen as we drove past speaker stands that looked like greymetal corn plants head high with microphones for ears. On the good screen the words "The Screen Explodes"—and the word 'explodes' had been written in a way to look that it was really exploding out from the screen—"With Action and Suspense," flashed out above the little kids, whose mothers were all yelling at them and trying to get them away from the playground and whose fathers were all smoking cigarettes in the car, leaning forward with their foreheads against the steering wheel, like they were very tired.

Most of the kids had fastened onto the bars of the swing sets and were going to have to be pried off like starfish.

Mama found a slot right up between the two screens and backed the truck in cab-headed east so Gretchen and I could prop up in the back and watch the west screen and she could sit in the front and watch the boring movie. They let you do that. I leaned over, plucked off one of the cornmetal speaker boxes, and shoved the handle that is supposed to go over the window down into the hole where the truck sideboards go.

Then you turn the knob a little...

"NEVER BEFORE HAS THE BIG SCREEN COME ALIVE! ALIVE WITH ACTION! ALIVE WITH THRILLS! ALIVE WITH..." "Turn it down, Katie!" said Mama, kind of loud because you had to talk loud because I had turned it up kind of much. She got out and came back to where we were.

"Turn it down!"

"Awwwwwww. We have to hear it!"

"We also have to hear other things after it's over." I don't know what she meant by that.

"Now. What do you guys want?"

"Hot dog."

"Hot dog."

"Popcorn."

"Small popcorn apiece."

"No! Big popcorn. Tubbapopcorn."

"Snowcone."

152

"Snowcone."

"Pickle."

"Pickle."

"Candy. Can we get candy?"

"M&M's! Big M&M's!"

"Be quiet. I shouldn't have asked. Here." She gave me a five dollar bill.

"Wow! We can use all of this?"

"Yes, except that you have to bring me a cup of black coffee and a hot dog. On my hot dog Katherine Marie I want a slender trail of mustard exactly bisecting the weenie. Is that clear?"

"Yes."

"More ruins it. Now go."

We jumped down out of the back of the truck and worked our way through the cars back toward the concession stand. It was a long, low building painted light green. From one end came this giant shaft of light that was the west screen movie and it just kind of hung there, a smoky white movie tube, so that every now and then teenagers would walk under it and jump up and poke their hands into it, which would then become the movie preview with hand shadows down by Robin Hood's foot.

"Look! There's Jason Bellamy!"

"Did you know that his sister smokes?"

"Yes. Annette Rogers smokes, too."

"How do you know?"

"Saw her."

"Where?"

"The filling station."

"She was probably just *holding* it."

"Uh uh, she was smoking it."

"She's gotta be like what, eleven?"

"Yes but her brothers are all such thugs. Her sister's a thugette."

"*Mean* it."

We turned down the ramp into the concession stand.

It was kind of filthy like concession stands at drive in movies always are, I don't know why but they are. In front of the actual counter where you filed by and got your stuff were long white kind-of-bars, kind-of-tables, about chest high, bolted to the floor, littered with crumpled up mustard stained napkins. There were two junior high school girls dressed up in elf uniforms trying to keep the bars clean; but those bars had been snackbarwitchcrafted and would always have, like, a styrofoam coffee cup with one cigarette butt floating in about an inch of I-guess-it's-coffee-but-please-never-let-it-get-close-to-my-mouth; or four little balsa wood stirring sticks; or two of the cardboard trays with circular holes at each corner to put cokes into—they would always have stuff like that pasted down by a blob of mustard or ketchup, no matter how many elf-girls looked mean and mad like they were saying bad things under their breath and kept carrying handfuls to the dumpsters out back.

"What are we gonna get?"

"I don't know. We have five dollars."

"I have to have at least two hot dogs. I'd rather have three but I *have* to have at least two. If I don't get three hot dogs then I want popcorn."

"Did you not get dinner?"

"Uh huh I had dinner, but it was roast or something yucchy. Look! Look at that bag of M&M's!"

"Wow! That's the biggest bag of M&M's I ever saw!"

"It must be twenty pounds of M&M's!"

"What'll we drink?"

"Coke! No! No! No! No! No! No! Root beer!"

"Yessss—"

"Oooooohhh! Look at the pickle jar!"

"Oh man, they're thick as roasting ears!"

But the hot dogs looked the best. The weenies rotated very slowly on hot chrome tubes, so that drops of weeniejuice popped and shined and made you just want to grab that weenie and ram it into your mouth.

It took us two trips to get all the stuff back to the truck, and when we finally got it done the movie had already started. That was OK though, because we had good stuff. We had four hot dogs, a tub of popcorn—not really a 'tub' of course, but a pasteboard bucket as big as the pail Mama and I put eggs in—three big pickles that we laid out on napkins between us, and two root beers. Mama was mad because she said I drowned her hot dog in mustard. It was hard, though. There was a huge bottle of mustard at the end of the counter, with one of those plunger things on top that you have to push down to make it blurt out. The problem is the first blurt just blurts air and a few drops of some kind of liquid that isn't mustard at all, but then you push hard and the second blurt blurts a full *mustard* blurt that globs all over the hot dog. Anyway she said not to worry and she could use the fork of her Swiss Army knife and eat it like a weenie casserole but to be more careful next time.

When we got all settled in and the food arranged the movie was at that place where they were getting funny bleeps on the radar.

All good monster movies begin when they're getting funny bleeps on the radar and the commander—he's the commander of a submarine or radar station on the coast or war airplane, depending on what kind of monster it is—stubs out his cigarette and looks real worried and says, "How could something that big move that fast?"

Pretty soon they were out on the beach. You just knew something was going to happen. There was a sheriff who said he was going to go down the beach and see if anything was behind those big rocks and there were the man scientist and the girl scientist who, even though they argued a lot, you could tell really liked each other, and then kissed each other right there on the beach, but agreed to stop because if the lab tests showed that the shiny stuff on the sand really was what they thought it was—octoplasm, I guess—it would be the end of the world.

Then the sheriff got killed.

"Ooohh. I wouldn't want to be that sheriff."

"I know. Look at how he's laughing."

"He thinks they're crazy, warning everybody that a giant creature might exist."

"A lot he knows."

"Turn around! Look out at the ocean!"

"I can't believe he's lighting a cigarette!"

"His last cigarette."

"*Mean* it!"

"That dork. 'I'm not worried about anything as long as I've got *this* baby.' Right. What does he think that little revolver is going to do for him?"

"Look at the ocean! Look at the..."

"Oh! Oh! Oh! There it is!"

"He doesn't see it!"

"Look around Superdork! Look around!"

"What a tentacle!"

"It must be a *hundred* feet long!"

"It must be a *thousand* feet long! Look at it waving up there in the air!"

"He doesn't see it! Aha! *Now* he sees it!"

"Serves him right! Look at his face!"

"Oh good, now try and *shoot* it."

"Turn around and run you idiot! Don't throw the gun at it!"

"I can't believe it! That thing must weigh a billion tons and he throws that gun at it!"

"Don't go backwards! Don't go… yep! Tripped on a root!"

"Oh, gross."

"Octopussed."

"Why do you suppose they always trip on a root?"

"I don't even know what a root is *doing* out there on the beach. Oh yucchh look the other two are kissing again."

"They said they wouldn't *do* that anymore! Don't they know what's going on down at the other end of the beach?"

"Pass the popcorn, please."

"No fair, you're getting more than I am."

"Am not."

"Are too."

"Besides, there's not enough butter on this popcorn."

"Sometimes there is. It's in, like, layers."

"Well I haven't found enough layers. Look. You've got mustard on your shirt."

"Oh gross. I hate it when it runs out of one end like that."

So anyway the monster wound up in San Francisco, which, when we told Mama about it later on, said that was exactly where it belonged, but I have to say that's where I thought the whole movie got a *little* unbelievable.

I mean, a tyrannosaurus rex can do OK in a big city because it can walk and run and jump around. But this huge octopus just oomphed up and kind of *beached* itself under the San Francisco bridge, and all it could do after that was lie there and reach into the city with its tentacles.

Now how far could it reach, really?

And wouldn't people figure *out* how far it could reach; and wouldn't they stay just a few feet further away?

So it wasn't a bad movie; but it wasn't completely like you believed it all the way from first to end like *The Creature from the Black Lagoon*.

It ended about ten-thirty. Mama drove slow back to the farm, so that we almost went to sleep in the back of the truck. When we got home we put the mattress on the iron bed frame that we kept out in the yard for summer nights and then used our tool shed quilt for cover, on the nights when it got colder.

And this was a perfect night.

A no-wind, whitepowder frost in the morning, autumn night. It's very different on a night with a full moon. You know how, when the nights get cold in fall or winter, it can be so clear that the sky looks like it will break; that the stars are tiny jewels and the sky around them is dark blue glass, that, if it fell down on the ground, would just break into a million pieces, it's that frozen? And everything that is usually dark at night, scary at night, you-can't-quite-see-it-and-monsters-might-be-hiding-there at night—everything is moonlight. Almost like covered in snow. The tree in the corner of the yard, the corn, the truck and tractor in the shed—all snow covered, like you could play at midnight and not be worried about a thing.

"Are you asleep?"

"No."

"Do you know what?"

"What?"

"Let's stay up tonight."

"Ooooohhh. Good idea."

"But are you sleepy?"

"No, not at all."

"I'm not either."

"Then we'll stay up all night?"

"Yes!"

"And we'll count the meteors?"

"Right! We'll count the meteors."

"How many is the most meteors we've ever counted before?"

"Fifty."

"No. A hundred."

"That's right! A hundred!"

"Tonight, if we stay up all night, we'll count a thousand."

"Or a million."

"Do you think we could count a million meteors?"

"Maybe. Maybe nobody's ever tried."

"Have you ever stayed up all night before?"

"Not really. Almost once. But I think I went to sleep. Because I remember it was like two AM, and then it was morning."

"That's not staying up all night."

"I guess not."

"But we'll stay up all night tonight, won't we?"

"Yes, we will."

"We'll make that promise to each other."

"Good. I promise."

"I promise, too."

"And if one of us goes to sleep, the other one will wake her up."

"And if that one won't wake up, the other one will throw cold water on her head."

"Do you know what's funny?"

"What?"

"Grownups."

"What about grownups?"

"Because, you know, when you tell them you want to sleep out, and they let you, but they kind of laugh like they think you'll come in about midnight?"

"Uh huh."

"And then you tell them that this time you're going to stay up all night—that you know you can do it, and you're not sleepy at all, and everything is just right, and you're not sleepy at all you're not sleepy at all and you'll never go to sleep never go to sleep never go to sleep no matter what—then they just look at you in that strange grownup way, and shake their heads like they know something that you don't know—and say: 'We'll see,'—and walk away."

We were quiet for a while. Then Gretchen said: "Katie?"

"Yes?"

"Am I your best friend?"

"You're my best Texas friend."

"Who's your best friend really."

"You're my best Texas friend, really."

"No. Who's your best friend really?"

"Katie Douthat. She's in Vermont. When we were in Atlanta together they called us Katie Dee and Katie Haw."

"Will she come visit you sometime?"

"I hope so."

"Well. I'm glad I'm your second best friend, Katie."

"I am too, Gretchen." And then we started counting meteors. I don't know how far we got. But I wish that you had been there to help us, Katie Dee. Come visit soon.

Katie Haw

Jenny

Jenny

January 7, 1968
Midlothian, Texas

Dear Katie Dee,

This was the Christmas I got Jenny. It wasn't like I thought it would be. It wasn't Mama telling me one afternoon, "Here, Katie, here's your lamb." It was a lot more special than that, and still is. I had been dreaming for so long about a lamb— about when the mother dies, and you take a coke bottle and a nipple, and it's your lamb, and it runs like crazy to you every afternoon and almost knocks the coke bottle out of your hand— I had been dreaming of that for so long, that when I tell you how I feel about Jenny, and what happened—you'll think I'm crazy. But she's still my lamb, and the best I could ever want.

I better start at the first.

It got really cold about ten days before Christmas. A norther came down from the panhandle, and the sky got gray, and fall ended. Just ended. No more leaves, no more of that trick or treating October weather when the sky is clear at night and the sun makes everything all golden in the afternoons—but sad gray, to cry, and drippy rain, slush, almost ice. The wind howled for two days, so that no matter how tight you tried to close the windows the cold still seeped in. Driving out to the farm, you couldn't see any color, anywhere. The way the world is in dead winter, when it will never be summer again. The fields the color that isn't any color at all, like the straw in an old wet haystack— and in between the fields mud roads and above the roads a mud

163

sky, your breath coming out of your mouth like fog.

Mama picked me up at school. You could hear sleet rattling on the top of the truck.

"Your math go OK today?"

"No."

"Why not?"

"I don't know. I just couldn't do it. I hate long division."

"We need to work on it then."

"I don't see why I need it. If I'm going to raise horses, why do I need long division?"

"We'll work on it."

It was that kind of a day.

We got home and changed clothes and then it was time to go down and put up the sheep. Sometimes, when it's really winter, the sun hardly comes up at all. At ten o'clock recess you see it just above the water tower in town, and you can look straight at it, because it's just a circle part of the clouds, a little whiter than they are gray—then when you come home, it's almost dark.

While we were walking down the dirt road toward the barn it started sleeting again.

We worked fast putting out feed. While the sheep were running in to get around the troughs Mama nudged me:

"I want you to watch the circle-eye ewe, Katie."

"With the black ring around her eye?"

"Yeah. She's ready, I think. We'll pull her out and put her into that side stall."

"How can you tell?"

"The way she walks. Watch her."

The circle-eye ewe had stayed back, and was walking to the end of one of the troughs where there was a space, but not much feed.

"Look at the way she walks!"

I slogged on across the getting crunchy manure and water and black marble sheep dropping mess that was the lot, and she and I caught the ewe and put her into her own stall. We got a little ground corn for her, and made sure she had fresh water. Mama caught her again, straddled her hip bones, and pulled her stub of a tail up.

"See her old behind here? See how red it is, and swollen? She'll lamb tonight. Now come on; let's go eat."

After supper she turned on a tape of the French Christmas Carols she likes. They're not bad. You get tired of "Deck the Halls with Boughs of Holly," whatever that means. I couldn't understand the French words either, but, as long as you're not going to understand Christmas song words, one language is as good as another.

Then we decorated our tree. We had cut it in the pasture the day before, but hadn't had time to put decorations on. It's a good thing to do, decorate the tree, because we have decorations that friends have given us. I have the owl that you sent me; it's a special decoration.

We went to bed a little after ten o'clock. Then we decorated our tree. About three hours later—I think it was one in the morning—Mama woke me. She scared me a little too, standing by the bed, shaking me, her slicker dripping on the covers. You could tell her hair was wet, and water lines streaked on her face.

"I need you."

"What? What is it?"

"I need you. Come on."

She never wakes me, so I knew it was pretty bad. Outside, the sleet came down harder, shaking the bedroom window frames. The wind howled like it was some big animal. My jeans and sweater were on a chair by the window, so it didn't take me long to get into them.

165

"What is it, Mama? Why did you go out?"

"I had to go down and check on the ewe."

"Did she have the lamb?"

"She's trying to. Come on. Let's go."

My slicker was in the mud room. I was still groggy, and had to run water in the mud room sink to get sleep out of my eyes. On the floor a lantern burned, and beside it was bucket of grease.

"She's having trouble, is that it?"

"Yeah."

"Shouldn't you call a vet?"

"You don't do that for sheep. He wouldn't come."

"But it's our ewe."

"He'd charge more to come than the ewe is worth. You don't call a vet for a sheep."

"Is she going to die?"

"I don't know."

"What do you want me to do?"

"I want you to stop asking questions. Come on."

The wind almost tore the screen door off. It made your clothes feel as though they weren't there, and it wasn't just cold, it was hurting cold. We had to lean over our steps as we walked, while by us in that black dark the doors of the sheds and out-buildings whammed and banged and screeched like owls on rusted hinges. Little needlesleet stuck you under your eyes, and around your mouth, until I thought I must have a thousand pricks of pimple and blood where it could get at my face.

Mama bent down close, so her legs got tangled with mine, and her breath warmed my ear; the lantern kept getting in the way between us, but it was all we had to see, and we had to stay in its little circle of light. The trees, getting ice covered now, groaned and snapped above us.

The sheep had gotten under the barn. They made no noise

at all, or maybe the wind, and the hayloft door banging, kept me from hearing. But their green eyes were like a bunch of winter fireflies under the barn, frozen in the cold, not moving, watching us as we slipped down from the road and through the gate.

"Move it, You! Get away, sheep."

We had to pull them aside to get through to the stall where we had penned the circle-eyed ewe.

The dry manure that was the floor had gotten so thick that it made the roof lower. We had to pull the shed door up to scrape it open. Mama set the lantern in the corner, while we took our slickers off. It was so cold I could hardly feel my fingers, so I kept blowing on them—my gloves were covered with a thin sheet of ice, and when you threw them down they crackled.

The ewe lay in the corner opposite.

"OK, come here Katie."

"Is she going to die?"

"I don't know. Probably."

The ewe lay on her side. Her eyes were swollen, white, bulging out. Mama took the lantern and set it by the shed wall. The two bell sacks glowed yellow.

"Pump it, will you?"

"All right."

She was rolling up her sleeves. She had on a short sleeve white blouse and didn't seem cold at all. Sweat on her forearms glowed in the lantern light. I didn't see how she could not be cold, because I was shaking.

I took hold of the knob at the lantern base and pumped several times, making the sacks glow white; the circle of light in the shed widened, and the black eyed ewe kicked once, and grunted. The kick scooted her back toward the wall of the stall; she kicked again, harder, so that her hooves banged against the boards. That scared her; she started lurching to get up, and Mama leaned down hard on her front hips until the sheep quieted down.

That was when I looked back. There was blood and filmy guck oozing out of her behind; but there was a black knot of something too, wrapped in a shiny kind of jelly. It took me a minute to recognize that it was the lamb's head. I just sat and stared at it, while Mama greased her hands and wrists with lubricating grease and got into position straddling the ewe's back legs.

You could see the slits that were the lamb's eyes, closed tight, just lines in the wet jelly sack.

"Is he alive?" I whispered.

"Probably not. Now come here. Sit on her; no, like that. Get your legs over her—straddle her, hold her head down hard. She's going to buck; keep her still."

"All right."

I put one hand on the neck of the circle-eyed ewe, and another on the top of her head, just above the ring around her bulging eye. She stayed quiet; some of the sheep in the barn outside the shed were bleating, thinking we were there to feed them.

Then Mama moved behind me. There was a sucking noise and the ewe lurched up under me, raising me off the ground and almost throwing me off.

"Hold her, Katie!"

"I can't!"

"Do it!"

"She's too strong!"

Mama gasped while she talked, and the ewe wrestled and pawed under me; I got my balance again and pressed down on her with everything I had, mashing the side of her face into the ground. The sucking noise came again—I held her better this time, because I knew which way she would kick.

Mama's shadow twisted, and turned; it was as though she was trying to lift a heavy weight, and kept straining, choking, gasping again for breath.

I guess it wasn't more than a minute, but it seemed like longer, that I had to sit there pressing the sheep's face down, rubbing it in the manure, listening to the sounds behind me.

"Quit. Get up."

I did. Mama bent over double. Her arm dripped blood and afterbirth, but the lamb's head hadn't moved.

"Sit down."

I did, against the far wall. Every few seconds the ewe grunted, kicked, and lay still again.

"I can't get it."

"Why doesn't it come out?"

Mama sat still for a time, breathing hard. Then she said:

"The way this is supposed to happen is that the head and two forefeet come out of her first, all at once, the head kind of wedged between the two hooves."

"What happened here?"

"Sometimes nature just doesn't do right. This time the head and one hoof came out. Look. You see it there?"

"I see the head."

"If you look close you'll see the hoof down beside it."

"I don't want to look that close."

"You have to."

"What?"

"You're going to have to take the lamb out, Katie."

"Mama, I can't."

"You have to."

"But didn't you say she's going to die anyway? And the

lamb, too?"

"I said probably. Right now the ewe is alive. Probably not the lamb, but the ewe is alive."

"Can't you just pull the lamb out of her?"

"No. That would kill her. She'd bleed to death in a minute or so."

"But how can I do it if you can't?"

"Your hand is smaller than mine."

"But I don't know how!"

"Come on. Let's get this lamb out."

"Mama—"

"Come on. Take your sweatshirt off."

I did.

"Now, roll up your sleeves; here, let me rub this on you. There you go."

She had a glob of orange lubricating grease and she lathered it all over my hand and arm.

"Listen: take the flat of your hand, lay it over the lamb's head. Then slide it right back down the neck, and force your hand inside her. You have to get it in there—the whole hand, up to your wrist."

She stood behind me, her arm around me, rubbing the grease up and down my arm.

I just nodded.

"Then you've got to crook your index finger—crook it, just like this—make a little hook of it, see?"

"Yes "

"The lamb's other leg is bent back. It's bent back at the knee, and bent under the lamb. That's why that leg can't come out. You've got to get your finger under the knee, and pull with your finger as hard as you can, so that the leg straightens out under the lamb. You've got to pull the second leg out of the ewe!"

"All right."

"Let's do it. I'll hold her. Do the job now, Katie. Get it done."

I got down on my knees and put my left hand on the upper part of the ewe's back leg. Then I cupped my right over the head, which felt like a wet softball under my palm.

"OK. You ready, Katie?"

"Yes, I'm ready."

"Get your hand inside her."

Leaning down hard I worked my fingers back down the lamb's neck, and snaked them up inside the ewe's behind; she snorted and struggled, and I could barely keep straddling her; I knew I was killing her, because blood spurted out on my wrist, and her squishy guts and insides slid like a bucket of no dirt, just earthworms, around my knuckles and between my fingers.

"That's good. Now find that knee."

"I can't—I can't move my hand around."

"Find the knee."

"Mama—"

"Find it."

My fingers opened and closed, more blood spurting, her hoofs crazy and kicking dried manure so that the cloud of it hung in the air. She kicked my shins, and my feet scrambled and worked to get between her legs that kept driving and kicking.

"You feel it?"

"No, it's just—I'm killing her!"

"Keep looking."

My hand slid down inside her; she lunged forward with both of us on her. Her hoof tore down my shin. I couldn't help from crying and pulling back; my hand sucked out of her. Doubled like a ball, crying—blood dripped off my right hand, and you could see it begin to soak though the blue jean leg where the hoof had ripped the skin above the shin.

"Here. Take this towel. Put it around your leg."

"Mama she kicked me so hard—"

"She's dying. Of course she kicked hard."

"I can't do this anymore."

"Take a couple of minutes. Then we'll quit if you want to."

"What about her?"

"She'll die soon, anyway."

"Shouldn't you—I don't know, shouldn't you bring the gun down and shoot her?"

Then Mama turned around and looked at me, real hard, and shouted. She never shouts at me, but this time she did:

"I don't know, Katie! I don't know whether to shoot her or let her die like this! Who am I, *God*?"

She stood there for a minute, then shook her head and sat down. After the first rag around my leg was soaked, I wrapped another, and then it wasn't bleeding so much.

Sleet came in waves against the shed roof. The other sheep had crowded up against the stall; their wool stuck in tufts through the slat plank wall.

"Hold her again," I said.

She didn't say anything, but just got up, and straddled the ewe's head.

"All right. I'm ready here. Do it."

Get the head; slide the hand—be ready for the lurch when—there it is, inside, soft and guts, all warm, move your finger, the first. . .finger, where is it, where is it, where—there."

. . . y . . es.

"You have it?"

"Yes."

Rock hard. Little knee. I'm under it, I know I am. Yes. Knee.

172

Under part of the knee, get under it, bone bone bone hard, finger crook, knee. Bone.

"You have it."

"Yes," I whispered.

"Pull."

"I can't…"

Won't come. Rock knee. Jammed in there. Just my finger how can I…

"Pull."

"I can't… get it…. I…"

Finger. Finger, pull finger get it….

Then, it came.

"Oh, yes!"

Plop, and a little blob of blood, and the little hoof, popping out of her. The ewe shook all over, and I knew, right there, in those seconds, she died.

"Pull the lamb out now! Get it out! Get it out! Get it out now!"

I could get both hands wrapped around its front shoulders now; I pulled hard, as hard as I could, and the whole thing came sliding out, a black and slippery sack of lamb.

"Good girl!"

Yes. Yes, yes, yes.

It was just there, at my feet, the long snake red cord, all the afterbirth.

And I was sitting, on my behind, just feeling it in my lap.

"Here, Katie," Mama whispered. "Here."

She had a sack. She took the lamb's body—because I knew that the lamb had to be dead, too—over by the lantern. I got up. I walked around, and knelt down by the ewe's face, and felt of it. It was just stone dead. A little blood came out of its mouth now. After a while Mama came over and put her arms around me.

"You need to get up and walk around, Katie."

"Yeah."

"You did good."

"Uh huh."

"The ewe is dead, girl. One of those things."

"I know."

"Come on. Get your slicker on. Let's go back to the house."

"Do we—"

"I'll bury her tomorrow. Let's go back now."

"All right." I felt—I don't know how to describe the way I felt. My legs wouldn't work. Mama helped me get my slicker on.

"I don't need it."

"You need it."

And it was true. I did need it, but—I was hot. I was shaking, and I was hot.

"I just—I just can't stop shaking."

"I know honey."

"Mama..."

"Yes?"

"Can I bury the lamb?"

"No, Katie."

"I mean— I want to. It's my lamb, you know? I mean, you can bury the mother but I want to bury the lamb. Will you let me?"

She looked down at me, and smiled, and put her hand under my chin.

"All right, darling," she whispered. "It's your lamb, and you can bury it."

"Thank you. Mama it's—it's Jenny. I know it's crazy to name it, but..."

"It's not crazy, honey."

"To me it's Jenny. And I want to make a grave for her—I know it's a 'her'."

"Yes. It's a 'her.'"

"And I want to bury her. . . Jenny. My lamb."

Then she just kind of rubbed her hand over my hair, and said, "You can bury your lamb, if you want to."

"I do."

"Then you can do it."

We listened to the storm for a while. She kind of laughed, and said:

"You might want to wait until it dies first."

I was crying then. I grabbed her, and cried into her chest. Then I pushed back, realizing I hadn't really heard her.

"What?"

"I said, 'Let's wait until Jenny dies before we bury her."

"Mama..."

"Come here."

Together we walked to the corner of the stall, where she had piled three or four burlap sacks. Jenny was lying on them, the afterbirth cleaned off now.

Her head moved back and forth, an inch one way, an inch the other. And her sides moved inside as she breathed.

Mama took my little finger. She pushed my finger inside the lamb's mouth.

"Come on, lamb," she whispered.

And, ever so soft, I could feel Jenny sucking at the tip of my little finger.

"Can she... I mean, if we get a coke bottle and some warm milk, will she..."

Mama shrugged. "How do I know? I'm not God."

But then she smiled, and rubbed her hand through my hair.

"But I'm betting on Jenny. Now come on. Let's take her home."

I carried her all the way, and couldn't sleep at all that night because of shaking, and trembling, and crying sometime and laughing sometime, and going in to where Jenny was sleeping in front of the fire until Mama said I couldn't go in there anymore.

That night Jenny put her tongue into a saucer of warm milk. The next day she nursed from the coke bottle. Not much, but enough.

And ten days later, Christmas Eve, was the first day Mama let Jenny out. The weather had gotten clear by then; I remember, I had to stay late for choir, so it was night when I got home. I got out of the truck, and the night was crystal clear and cold as black glass—and up came Jenny, with a bell around her neck, rubbing up to my leg and wanting her bottle.

And that was the best Christmas present I could ever have gotten.

Come visit soon, Katie Dee.

Your best friend still,

Katie Haw